BEAUTY AND THE PROFESSOR

SKYE WARREN

CHAPTER ONE

ERIN

ERIN RODRIGUEZ JOGGED up the steps of the farm-style house in good spirits.

She let herself in using her key and called out, "Mr. Morris! It's Erin."

Call me Blake, he always said, but for some reason she couldn't. She wasn't usually a stickler for propriety, but with him it seemed like a good idea. Maybe his military roots made the formality seem right to her. Or more likely, it was the domesticity of cleaning his home. The barrier of his last name was little defense against her attraction.

It would be so easy to slip, to let him see how she felt about him. Then she'd feel like an idiot—a hopeless little girl dreaming about a man old enough to be her father.

She pulled a book from her bag and went upstairs in search of her boss. The pages were well-worn when he gave it to her. Even more so after she read it. Three times. She could probably put it in his bookcase, always neat and organized so she'd know right where it belonged. In fact, his whole house sparkled from the knotted floorboards to the arched ceilings.

It was partly because he was neat, but also because she came twice a week. It was one of the odd habits that made her reclusive employer so strange, and also endearing.

He never left a mess, but he didn't want her to come less.

Not that she should complain. She needed the hours.

Well, she could replace the book on her own, but she wouldn't. The truth was that she wanted an excuse to talk to him. They'd had a lively debate on the merits of the U.N. in her political science class yesterday and she knew he'd appreciate the highlights.

Blake Morris used to be a professor at Tanglewood University, before he went on one last tour in the Middle East. Before he was hit with an IED and burned over thirty percent of his body. Since then he'd lived in seclusion, not teaching, barely ever leaving his house, but she saw the textbooks with his name on them.

She poked her head in his bedroom and found

him there.

In a manner of speaking…

Her breath caught in her throat as she took in the sight. He lay spread out on the bed, his skin still damp from a bath, a white towel fallen open around his waist. The tanned skin and flexing muscles. The fist he made. Oh God. She couldn't focus.

And he was masturbating. *Shit!*

This was so bad. And strangely beautiful. He was like some Adonis. Old-world artists would have wanted to create a statue out of marble. She ought to leave. This was clearly a private moment. He wouldn't want her to see this. Not only because of his obvious nakedness, but because of the scars she could see—they continued down the side of his face, his neck, onto his muscled torso, the outside of his thigh.

She really should turn around, walk away and absolutely, positively not watch. Instead she stood there, her eyes riveted to his exposed cock standing up thick from his fisted hand.

"God, baby," he moaned, his eyes closed. "Suck it, please."

Her lips parted in surprise, as if she could obey him from across the room. Her sex throbbed to hear his rasping voice say those dirty words, to watch his hand fuck his cock. It was shocking and invasive and so compelling that she wanted to fall to her knees.

"Yes. *Yesss*. So beautiful. God." His other hand reached to cup his balls. "That's right, baby. Lick them. Suck them."

Her gaze flew to his face, mesmerized by the interplay of shiny, scar tissue and ruddy, healthy skin twisted in a grimace of pleasure. His burns and coarse features might make him intimidating to some people, but when she looked at him she saw only Blake, with his brilliant ideas and gruff kindness, with his harsh sensuality.

"Touch yourself. Yeah, yeah. Take me deep in your mouth and stick your fingers in your cunt. Make yourself feel good, beautiful."

His eyes were shut, lashes fanning over his masculine cheeks.

Who was he imagining kneeling in front of him?

Her thighs squeezed together where she stood, giving herself what relief she could. If she moved, either her legs or her hands, she'd have to acknowledge that what she was doing, that watching was wrong, so she stayed very still.

Then, shockingly, he moaned her name, "Erin…"

She barely had time to process that, and then he came, spurting into his cupped hand.

Her whole body clenched hard, not quite an orgasm, more like an echo. The suggestions of climax. An involuntary sound escaped her—a whimper, almost.

Heavy lids slid open as he turned to look at her. His eyes widened into a look of shock, even horror. He looked angry, and of course, of course he should be. He should be furious.

Mortified, she turned and ran down the stairs. The sound of her name hurtled down the steps after her, not in passion this time, but she couldn't go back. She invaded his privacy in the worst way. Maybe finding him had been an accident.

Staying had been unforgivable.

Even knowing that, she couldn't say she'd act differently.

Part of her wanted to run outside, to climb into her car and drive away. But she needed this job, if there was any hope of keeping it. Her scholarship covered tuition, but not the rent on her small apartment, not the electric bill or textbooks or gas to get to school.

And more than that, she needed to apologize to him.

Blake Morris had always been decent to her. Always kind.

He didn't deserve her ogling him.

Pacing in the kitchen, she battled her embarrassment at being caught in a compromising position. Or rather, she'd caught *him* in a compromising position. She'd have to face him, but she couldn't look for him. Not right then and maybe not ever. She would just have to live here in the kitchen, for ten minutes or ten hours.

For ten years, if that's how long it took for him to come downstairs.

Her hands caught on the stone edge of the countertops then smoothed across the surface. Already clean, as usual. She would run her rags over the shiny granite until it gleamed. That's what she should have done instead of looking for him. Why did she even think he'd be interested in hearing about her class? Or her thoughts about the book?

She'd never done anything quite this embarrassing. Watching the man's private moment? That was low. And even worse, she respected him, so much.

She *liked* him, and she might have ruined everything.

Nervous energy pumped through her veins.

She pulled out the cleaning supplies, thinking that at least she could turn her wild energy into something useful.

Blake bounded down the stairs, wearing sweatpants.

There was no towel. She couldn't help but admire him before, the way the thin fabric of his T-shirt hung on his well-built shoulders, loose around his abs, but now all she could see was his naked body in her mind.

As if she hadn't already proven herself a coward, she turned away to flee.

"Erin," he said in those low tones she felt to the bone. "Wait, please."

She paused and turned halfway back to him, willing the inappropriate, private, *sexy* images to subside. A reddened cock. Thick ropes of come. *God.*

"I'm sorry you had to see that," he said. "It won't happen again. I swear it," he said, as if he was the one who did something wrong. "Don't quit."

She'd never expected to see him like this, practically begging—not for anything, and certainly not for his maid to continue cleaning for him. Did she really vacuum so well?

No. If nothing else, today had shown that he

at least thought about her in another way. Is *that* why he kept her around, why he increased her cleaning schedule and chatted with her about his work? Should she be offended? But she wasn't offended.

Instead she was flattered and confused and aroused as hell.

She stammered, "I don't understand. Were you…was I…?"

He closed his eyes and lowered his head. "There's no excuse," he said, swallowing. "But I won't—" He broke off and looked away. The part of his face turned toward her was the more scarred half. That gesture more than anything showed his distress since he usually took pains to hide it. Who could think less of him, knowing he'd earned those scars in service to his country?

"What can I do so that you won't leave?" he asked.

"I—honestly, I hadn't even thought of quitting. Mr. Morris, I'm the one who needs to apologize. For intruding on your privacy. For watching you."

"Thank you," he said stiffly, either in acknowledgment of her apology or her agreement she didn't know. He paused then repeated, "I'm sorry."

After a curt nod, he left the room.

Everything was fixed, wasn't it? Except she felt bereft, as if something had been lost. Maybe she should have clarified that he hadn't done anything wrong, after all. But it would be too strange to correct him in his assumption. What could she say? *Please, go ahead and use me in your fantasies. I don't mind.* That would hardly make this situation less awkward.

Besides, she needed time to think, to process what she had seen and her feelings about it. Well, she'd just committed not to quit, whatever came of her thoughts.

Over the next few hours, she cleaned his house as usual. Blake seemed to stay out of her way, not lingering to chat with her about politics or history or to ask how school was going, as he often did. She left his bedroom for last and resolutely ignored the way her panties grew damp as she made his bed, imagining she could still feel the warmth of his body in the white sheets.

BLAKE

THANK GOD SHE hadn't left.

What a clusterfuck. As the minutes counted down on the clock, Blake Morris had known she would arrive. He couldn't seem to deflate his erection. The last thing he wanted to do was leer at her with a goddamn hard-on, so he'd gone to take a cold shower.

That hadn't even worked.

He needed to masturbate to bring it down. It was the only way to get rid of it. Erin couldn't see his inappropriate desire for her. It would ruin everything.

What happened was so much worse.

Of all the ways to lose her, that would've been the stupidest. Not that he *had* her, exactly, but seeing her twice a week and getting to talk with her was more than he deserved, and he was damned grateful for it. He chose not to analyze the pathetic factor of that.

It was shitty of him to use her work to bring her to his house. He'd never had such a clean house in his life. But he couldn't bring himself to stop seeing her, either.

Someone so beautiful and good had no business being around a goddamn coward like himself, but fuck if he wasn't selfish enough to force her anyways. Lord knew he had no good looks, no charm, and as evidenced by earlier, no intelligence with which to lure her instead.

In some circles he was known as a great mind

in military strategy.

The great intellectual, thinking with his dick.

Not that he didn't excuse himself to a certain extent—God, she was beautiful. Seeing her watching his dick while he'd come had only inflamed his lust for her, her cheeks pink, her lips parted, but it was best not to think about that or he'd get hard all over again.

It was bad enough to be scarred and ugly, broken in body and spirit, wasn't it? Surely he didn't need to add exhibitionist to his faults, flashing unsuspecting maids who didn't want him.

Chapter Two

Erin

ONE HOUR INTO her next cleaning visit, Erin was getting worried.

She wished everything could go back to normal, but Blake seemed to be avoiding her. He made a brief appearance to say hello. *Hello*, as if they were nothing more than employer and maid. As if he hadn't made her laugh and hope and develop a massive crush on him.

As if he hadn't been masturbating with her name on his tongue.

He didn't sit on the couch as she folded the clothes or lean against the bookshelves while she dusted. He didn't tell her about what book he was writing, what article he was researching, didn't ask about her classes.

Normally he wore a soft T-shirt and sweatpants, the kind made thin from many washes. He worked from home and preferred to be comfortable.

Today he wore jeans and a white collared shirt.

Nothing about this was normal.

This new formality had to be a reaction to the incident from last week. Perhaps he felt violated or unsafe with her. *Can you blame him?* She had basically ogled him.

Guilt serrated her insides.

It didn't help that she had explicit dreams about him and his cock two nights in a row. Dreams where he said those same words, but she was there, naked beside him, and she did what he commanded. Masturbating to thoughts of each other was a contagious condition, one she'd apparently now caught. If he could walk in on her touching herself, they'd be even.

Blake ducked out of the kitchen with a glass of water at the exact same moment she entered from the other side. This couldn't continue, could it? She wouldn't make him uncomfortable in his own home.

"Mr. Morris."

He stopped and turned, his unscarred side towards her. "Hey, Erin."

She softened her voice, almost pleading. "I want to apologize again for what happened last time, Blake." If using his first name was the price of his forgiveness, then she would gladly pay it. "I should have left right away when I saw what you were doing…well, I was just surprised." *And more turned on than I've been my entire life.*

He cleared his throat. "Apology accepted."

Except it didn't *feel* accepted, not when he couldn't look her in the eye. He gave her what she supposed was an encouraging smile but looked more like a grimace. And *that* made her think of what he looked like when he climaxed. *Damn it.*

She really should shut up now, but she couldn't seem to stop. "I was wondering if you…that is, you *were* thinking of me, weren't you? There wasn't some other Erin?"

His jaw clenched. Hard. "There's no other Erin."

"Well, it's only that, I wondered if…if it was just a passing thought or if it was more…"

He looked alarmed now, and she cursed herself silently. "Erin," he said, his voice hoarse. "You don't feel that I was asking you to do any-thing…inappropriate, do you? That I would try to make you do something—something you didn't want? That was never my intention."

"No!" she exclaimed in dismay. "Of course not. I just meant that, well, if you *were* interested in me that way, well, I—" She took a deep breath and rushed out, "I wouldn't necessarily be opposed to it."

"You—" He broke off. She noticed detachedly that his hand was gripping the counter so tight his knuckles were white. He swayed forward as if to approach her but then leaned back. "You're not opposed to it."

Her cheeks burned at a thousand degrees. "I want you to do what you said."

"God." He wasn't avoiding her eyes anymore. That dark gaze burned into hers. "Are you sure you don't feel pressured? I would never *ever* want you to feel that you had to—"

"No, no. It's not that, I swear. And the same goes for you, too. If you don't want to, *please* don't feel that you have to, you know, actually *do* anything with me—"

"If I don't want to," he repeated, sounding dazed.

His eyes turned unfocused before they pinned her. He circled her, moving to stand behind her. Awareness raised goosebumps on the back of her neck. Her hair rustled where his face leaned into her hair, as if he were scenting her.

"If I don't want to," he said again, almost tasting the words. "How would that work? How would it be possible to not want you? To not dream about you?"

He trailed a finger lightly from the crown of her head, down her hair, along her shoulder and her arm. It was almost a whisper touch, not overtly sexual, but she found the suggestion more erotic than a firm grasp. The past two days of heightened arousal boiled over until she felt saturated with need, heavy and too hot.

"Please," she whimpered, shocked even as she said it.

Erin had always been too proud, to her detriment. Her circumstances, cleaning houses while her classmates drove their BMWs to class, struggling to pay rent while they used their parents' black credit cards, ought to bring her down, but she refused to be cowed.

She never begged, not for anything, money, favor, and certainly not sex. Yet here she was wanting—no, *needing* him, a feeling foreign but very real.

And he seemed to need her right back.

"God, yes," he breathed against her temple. "I want to touch you."

"Like before," she said, her voice wavery. That had only been a dream—something in his imagination that had come alive in hers. A shared fantasy. This would be real.

"Come upstairs." He held out his hand, and it felt like so much more than an afternoon. It felt like he was promising her pleasure and sweetness and everything her heart desired.

She put her hand in his, her heart squeezing with anticipation and worry.

They passed the bathroom, where the countertops still gleamed from the last time she was here. Reality intruded in heavy stomps—*that's what I'm here to do, to clean his house, not have sex.* What would it make her if she got paid for this hour?

It took effort to force the idea away. Regardless of what happened next she wouldn't accept money for today. And she would take this moment without apology to herself or anyone else. Couldn't she have this much? Every other minute was for work—to study and make good grades and pay for tuition. This minute would be something else.

He shut the bedroom door, closing them in.

No one else was in the house but the two of them, but it added to the intimacy of the moment, that closed door. This wasn't a chance encounter, but an illicit meeting. A joining. A decision. She glanced at the bed and swallowed hard.

Blake stepped behind her and buried his face in her hair. Amused, she made a mental note to stock up on this shampoo. Then the heat of his body and his own woodsy scent enveloped her, and she forgot everything else.

His hands rested lightly on her shoulders, then slid down to her breasts. He stroked them, only thin fabric between his hands and her flesh. Her breath caught. The gentle caress dipped to her waist and then beneath her shirt to touch bare skin. She wore yoga clothes when cleaning, comfortable to maneuver in but stretchy enough to allow him access.

He cupped her breasts beneath the elastic, circling and pinching her nipples until they ached. Pausing to draw her shirt and bra up over her head, he returned his hands to her breasts—thank God. Cool air wafted against her sensitive skin, a sharp contrast to his hands. His breath, hot and increasingly labored, blew against her shoulder. What a sight she must have made for him, her breasts bare and flushed.

"So lovely," he whispered.

He pinched harder, and pure sensation spiked through her core, making her moan. Her hips canted forward in search of friction, rubbing against nothing. In answer to her involuntary plea, he slipped his hand into the waistband of her pants—roaming lower and lower until he reached the curve of her mound, until he found her wet folds.

One long finger dipped down to her opening to draw the moisture up to her clit. His mouth worked along the side of her neck in light kisses and licks. Her head fell back to his chest as she abandoned herself to the pleasure. His fingers slid down into her folds and slipped inside, thrusting his fingers in as the heel of his hand pushed into her clit.

Her hips bucked as she mindlessly sought climax.

She came in a blinding whirl of pleasure, an almost unbearable relief, as if she'd been waiting to come since she saw him climax last week. Her whole body fell back against him, sated, boneless. The tension of these past few days, of these past few months, if she were honest, finally released. All her worry made quiet in one explicit moment.

He undressed her completely and placed her on the bed.

She had no strength to stop him. No desire to stop him. By the time she floated back down to earth she lay spread eagle on the bed, completely naked, with him kneeling between her legs. She only had a glimpse of his scarred face, taut and carnal with arousal, before he lowered his head and brought her to ecstasy again.

He brought her to climax four, five times—a generous lover. She lost count. He made her come again and again with his mouth on her clit and his fingers thrusting inside her.

"Yes, yes, that's it," he would moan when she came.

He was relentless in his pursuit of her orgasms, taking unmistakable pleasure in her sounds and responses. She was reminded of how they would discuss topics related to his work or her college classes. He always argued fiercely and often won their debates, but when she would win, he wouldn't look disappointed or angry—he looked almost proud. Triumphant, even. Like her victory was his, and now her ecstasy was his, too.

"You're beautiful," he murmured. "So damn beautiful. You look like a goddess. Like a warrior. Like you could slay me and you *do*. Just looking at you ruins me. I could watch you lying spread like this forever. Open to me, wet and flushed— forever and never grow tired."

She'd read his articles and treatises and inter- views. He had plain-spoken words and scientific words and even words of dry humor, but she had never heard these words before. These almost-poetry words melted her everywhere, sex and love made into sound.

Her body throbbed, exhausted from her climaxes, but her heart burst from his generosity. She wanted to do something for him. She wanted to do *everything* for him.

Erin reached down and touched his cock, drawing a gasp from him. The pulsing shaft jerked in her hand. He pulled away. From her position she couldn't reach him in his retreat. He touched her again and she jumped, oversensitive.

"Just let me please you," he said. "Let me give you pleasure." His caress lightened.

She moaned and her legs relaxed open again. It felt too good to question, too incredible when he had learned how to touch her in exactly the right way to make her come.

"Yes," he murmured. "Yes, that's right. Good girl."

His fingers spread apart her folds, slick and swollen. "I'll make you feel so much pleasure," he said. "So much you won't care that it's me."

Wait, what? She tried to push through the haze of her arousal.

"So good you'll forget it's me," he whispered, staring down at her spread legs, entranced. "You won't regret this. I won't let you regret this," he promised.

"Stop," she gasped out. "What—what did you say?"

He shook his head and some of the sensual fog cleared from his eyes. "I'm sorry," he said. "Did you…did you want to stop? Are you done with me?"

"No, I don't want to stop," she said, torn between exasperation and a deep tenderness for the man between her legs. "I want to keep doing this with you. Lie down."

He blinked in apparent surprise but moved to obey, his muscled body splayed on the bed. Like it had been that day she walked in on him, except now she could touch him.

Without giving him a chance to reject her, she reached down and grasped his cock again. He felt heavy in her hand, large enough to intimidate her—but he held so still. As if he didn't want to scare her. All the muscles in his body held tight, strong hands twisted in the sheets.

She touched her tongue to the tip.

"Oh God, *yes*," he groaned, just as he had when he'd pleasured himself with his hand, imagining her mouth. This time was real, and she'd make sure he knew it.

She savored the salty flavor as it hit her tongue, breathing in the musky, male smell of his groin. His thighs shook with restraint, especially when she pressed her lips to the crown of his cock in a chaste kiss. All this power and virility trembled under her mouth. It intoxicated her.

Erin took him deep and then pulled back to the tip. In and out.

Deeper and deeper.

The rhythmic motions of his cock sliding back and forth between her lips felt like a chant. This man was so good and so kind and yet...did he question his worth because of his scars? It was impossible. Those wounds, received in battle as a soldier, proved his bravery and honor. It was another example of him protecting others, the way he advocated for unheard groups and causes in his writing, the way he debated social justice.

How dare anyone—how dare *he*—question his value? He was everything she could ever want in a man. He was everything she wanted, and for this moment, he was here, in her hands. In her mouth. She loved him.

What the hell? Where had that thought come from?

No, she couldn't love him. There was no future for him and her.

Only now. Only this, his pulsing arousal between her lips. Her eyes snapped open to find him staring at her intently, as if he could devour her with sight alone. He looked fierce and sexy and intimidating. Her eyes widened at the hunger in his eyes.

Through his arousal, he managed a small smile and touched her cheek tenderly. "It's okay," he said softly. "You don't have to look."

He thought she didn't want to look at him, to see his beautiful face? He thought she wanted to pretend it was someone else licking her, pleasuring her?

Anger burned inside her like acid. Anger because he doubted himself. Anger because he doubted her, too, thinking that she'd be so shallow.

Anger at the faceless people who had wounded him, outside and in.

It didn't have to be like that. She would prove it to him. Even if this afternoon was all she had with him, he would know his worth to her.

A battle. That was what they'd have—a sensual battle to make him understand. She fought by tightening her lips and sucking hard. His hips bucked in helpless response, and he groaned, eyes closing, knuckles turning white as he clenched the sheets.

She continued her onslaught using strong suction and steady thrusts. She took him in deep, too deep. Almost hurting her throat, impaling herself with his cock; she didn't care. She sucked him that way as hard as she could, as if his cock was her lifeline—and maybe it was.

"Erin," he moaned. "It's too much. You have to stop. Oh fuck, don't stop." He thrust his hips up jerkily, mindlessly trying to get deeper, push farther.

She tried to oblige him, jamming her head down onto him, her lips grazing the hair at the base. And that groan rumbled all the way into her throat. She could have come from the sound alone, if her hands had been free to touch herself, but they weren't.

His cock choked her, but it seemed insignificant compared to this. Compared to the strain of his thighs beneath her palms, to the ache between her legs. He came with a hoarse shout and a burst of warm fluid down her throat, trembling for what seemed like hours but could only have been minutes, his body made supplicant by the flick of her tongue.

Violent shudders ran through him, even after she lifted herself from his cock, even when he reached down to grasp her, to pull her up, seeking a connection she was too willing to give. A similar sated haze crept over her. She clambered up his body and curled herself up at the crook of his arm, feeling like some small animal, a squirrel nestling in the cradle of a tree. Replete. Safe. He would hold her through the storm.

CHAPTER THREE

BLAKE

B LAKE ABSOLUTELY WOULD not, under any circumstances, jump her bones.

Not right away. No, not ever again. At the very least, it was sexual harassment, what he had done. His mind had even drifted to the worst in the days since she'd gone. What if she hadn't wanted it? What if she'd felt that she couldn't say no? It would have been practically rape.

Either way, he should be arrested. Beaten.

Someone should kick his ass for taking advantage of her. It was too damned bad that Erin didn't have anyone to beat the shit out of him. No father, no brothers, no punk-ass college boyfriend either. She was vulnerable, and he'd been the worst kind of bastard.

"Mr. Morris, it's Erin." It was the same way she always called out when she came into the house, and his cock hardened like a goddamn puppet on a string. *God, no.*

He couldn't do this. Bad enough she knew he was a dirty old man, taking advantage, lusting after her. Worse that he'd used her own desperation, her need to work to pay for her college, as a tether to keep her near him.

He couldn't also take her body, her innocence.

Isn't that what you did, asshole?

It was a little late to protect her when he'd already come down her throat.

No matter what he'd done to her, she *was* innocent. It didn't matter that he'd touched her. That her mouth made him come hard enough to see stars. Not even before his injuries had he gotten it so good. But her brown eyes were so open, so trusting. Her body was lithe and smooth and young. She was innocence personified. He didn't deserve any of it.

There she was, entering the kitchen. That incredible body and beautiful mind.

Everything he couldn't have. "We have to talk."

She picked up on his tone correctly, setting her face into solemn lines, but then she'd always been bright. Probably she was worried he'd touch her again, put his filthy hands on her body and his ugly face near hers. And why shouldn't she be worried?

"I'm afraid this isn't going to work," he said, damning himself for being an animal. If he'd been able to keep his hands to himself, he could have kept seeing her. "You can't work here anymore."

Emotions chased across her face—worry and fear and hurt. "Okay," she said, sounding calm. But her hands trembled around the broom she held. And when she saw that he'd noticed, she leaned it against the door.

She wasn't one to show her weakness, and he hated that he'd made her weak.

"You understand, this isn't any fault of yours. You've done a great job. I've never had such a clean house. It's just…well, I'm sure you realize the problem."

"Right," she said, her voice hollow. "I understand."

"It can't happen again." He didn't want to hurt her, but he could see that he had. She needed the money from this job. That much was clear from her threadbare clothes and secondhand textbooks. And maybe she would be a little disappointed. He liked to think they'd had a friendship, but maybe that had been in his head.

Maybe she'd be relieved that she could get away from the lecher without him making a fuss.

That would have been bad, but this was far worse.

"I know you rely on this job for college, and I'm not going to let my actions ruin that for you. I can give you some money. The same amount you would have made it if you'd kept working here. So you don't have to worry about that."

Her voice broke. "You want to pay me?"

"Well, yes," he said, confused that she seemed even more distressed. He was the one who fucked up, by having sex with her. He would pay the price in the worst possible way—by not seeing her again. The least he could do was leave her whole, and that meant paying her the wages she would have earned.

Her lower lip trembled. "You can keep your goddamn money."

"I don't understand. I thought you needed it."

"You don't understand? I'll explain it to you. I know I'm just some stupid college kid and you don't really care. I can accept that. I'm just a maid to you, and a girl you can fuck, fine. But I am not a whore. You can't have sex with me and then pay me to go away."

Shock left him breathless. "I didn't mean it like that. Of course you're not a whore."

Her face crumpled at the last word. She turned and ran from the room, her dark hair flying behind her. It took him only a second to follow. He caught up to her as she grabbed her purse from the hallway table, fumbling inside for her keys.

He touched her arm. "Erin. Erin, please."

She couldn't see what she was doing through her tears, and she dropped the bag in frustration, but she refused to look up at him. His chest ached at her clear distress.

"Erin, I'm sorry," he said. "I never should have touched you. You deserve so much better than this. Better than me—"

"Oh, don't give me that," she cried, finally turning up her tear-stained cheeks to him. "You know I'd give anything to be with you. I'd take it any way you could give it to me, but not if you're going to *pay* me for it. I can't be a prostitute, even for you."

"Never," he said, his jaw hard. "That's not what it would have been. I want you, that's all. I just can't have you. You're so beautiful, so young, and I—"

Her eyes were bright with unshed tears. "Shhh," she said, pressing a finger to his lips, a hitch in her breath. "That's it. That's all we need to say to each other. If you meant what you said, if you really want me, then that's enough for me."

"Well, it shouldn't be," he said, his voice hard. Anger made him meaner than he meant to be, colder than he thought he could. "You should have standards. You should—"

She took a step back and grabbed the hem of her shirt, and he forgot what he was going to say. She should—what? He couldn't think, especially when she lifted the shirt over her head.

Her bra was something made for working out, a bright purple. He didn't understand why it was so damned pretty. Straps crisscrossed over her cleavage, emphasizing the pretty curve. The thin, stretchy fabric gave him a clear view of her hard nipples. His mouth went dry with the urge to lick her, to taste her. To bite her until the soft flesh of her breasts trembled against him.

Warning bells clanged in his head. He'd said he wasn't going to do this, wasn't going to touch her, that he didn't get to have her.

Then she pulled off the pretty purple bra, too, and his brain shut off.

With a groan of surrender, of appreciation, he pulled her into his arms for a slow, languorous kiss, his tongue exploring hers with slow, insistent demand. This was happening. Whatever came after would be on his head, but for now he had to taste her, to feel her beneath him, to pretend that he was worthy of a woman like her.

Beautiful, beautiful. He wanted to touch her in all the beautiful places, but that was everywhere. Her full lips, but no, that was for him to explore. And those breasts, plump and tipped with bronze—they were for his mouth.

Lower was the soft, feminine curve of her stomach, all sleek lines and sloping shadows. And even lower, the satiny softness of her sex, but he couldn't touch all the places. Not at once, and that's what his mind was consumed with, now.

Touch her now, take her now. *She's mine now.*

Too late, he noticed her hand pressing against his chest, stopping him. She wanted him to stop. Yes, he would. Of course he would. He would never force himself on anyone, and especially not her. Not his broken face or his worn body.

She wasn't really stopping him. Instead she took him by the hand and led him upstairs to the bedroom, the same way he led her last time. Kicking off her black yoga pants, she crawled onto the bed, making him watch the curve of her ass.

Her legs were parted in that haphazard way of a woman. Sprawling in invitation but tilted closed with modesty. It was the perfect dichotomy that made her—the knowing seductress, the innocent young woman. He wanted them both.

Before he could process any reasons why he shouldn't, he was on top of her. A crazed man. He licked and sucked and *bit*. She should stop him, the small rational part of his brain demanded. That thought was doused by her heat and his.

She gave it all back to him. Touching him, tasting him.

Her mouth worked its way down, and he wanted that—God, did he. He wanted her to suck him again, but he couldn't last. He knew he couldn't, so he stopped her.

"Baby," he said, and she stopped and looked at him. He nudged her shoulder, not able to get out more words than just that. *Baby*. She was his.

ERIN

AT HIS URGING, Erin rolled to her hands and knees. Yes. This way, that way. The position didn't matter, so long as he got inside her, in her mouth or *somewhere*. She was frantic with it, with the need to hold him in her body.

The sharp tear of the wrapper, a short pause and then he was at her entrance. His cock thrust into her from behind, and she cried out at the stretch of him—bigger than she expected, more than she had ever taken before. It hurt, but she wouldn't have stopped him for anything.

He covered her with his body as if protecting her from some threat. There could be a bomb going off, and this is how he'd shield her. Only, the bomb was his lust—and he fucked her the same way he protected her. "Baby, you're so hot. Do you know how much I want you? All I can think about. You make me stupid. Mine, mine."

It felt good. It did. But…she thought back to the first time and what he had said. *You don't have to look.* Is that what he was doing? Making it so she didn't have to see him?

She wanted to see him.

More than that, she didn't want him to think she didn't. God, who had made him think that? He was a handsome man. The scars only added to that.

She started to turn, but he put a strong hand on her back, holding her in place.

"Not good?" he said, his breathing harsh, restrain a rough edge.

She could feel him changing the angle and—ahh!—yes, that was good, it was impossibly good. Her eyes rolled back. That wasn't the point though. That wasn't the problem.

She jerked away so he had no choice but to let her go or restrain her.

He let her go. He always would, she knew that.

He would always be gentle with her. Without giving him a chance to think, to pull away, she flipped over, spread her legs and guided his cock inside her. His eyes widened, as if he might protest, but then they slid shut.

He moaned, long and low. "So good. Mine."

She wanted to smile at that—she loved when he said that. She never wanted him to stop saying it, but she couldn't smile at all. Not when the pressure, the tension, the joy of it was building, higher and higher. She could hardly breathe, much less smile, and then she'd reached the peak. She came with a strangled cry, and he followed after, pumping into her and wringing out her orgasm until she was begging for him to stop.

"Erin," he mumbled into her hair. "Don't leave. Don't ever leave."

He froze. She could almost hear him thinking—first replaying what he'd just said and then searching for something to say. Some way to take it back.

She cupped his cheek in her hand. It was the one that fit her free hand, but it happened to be the damaged one, the scarred one, and she stroked her thumb over the too-smooth, discolored skin.

"I'm not going anywhere," she whispered.

He groaned and shut his eyes, turning his face into her touch.

Chapter Four

Erin

Two weeks later

ERIN WOKE UP in slow degrees.

Awareness tugged at her like a gentle tide. Arousal lapped at her skin. She had been in a deep slumber, both sated and sore, but she came alive again under his touch.

Blake. Sighing, she might have said his name aloud. Or maybe just in her mind. They were in sync right now, so soon after sex. Wrapped up in each other, cocooned in sleep. Past the point of discussions, negotiations, they'd been stripped to the core.

Just him, her, and the pleasure they could invoke together.

Calloused fingers roamed over her hips and lower, lower, to where her curls were still damp from their earlier sex. She turned her head toward the windows. A faint, eerie light glowed against the curtains, heralding late twilight, the onslaught of night. He was insatiable really. Earlier this evening, then now. They'd do it again in the morning most likely. She loved it.

When his fingers slipped inside the wetness pooling at her sex, she moaned.

"Shh. I didn't mean to wake you."

Liar. A lazy smile curved her lips. "Is that right?"

He found her clit and pinched. His breath was hot at the back of her neck, his erection pressing urgently against her from behind. "But now that you're up…"

"You have plans for me." Delicious plans. They always were.

"You don't have to do a thing," he murmured, rolling her onto her back. He nuzzled his way through the valley of her breasts, across her belly, and settled in between her legs. Her knees splayed wide, her whole body spread open to him, encouraged by anticipation and the laxity of sleep. Her hips canted up, an instinctual invitation.

She'd been given oral sex before, but never by someone as dedicated as Blake. He enjoyed himself as much as he enjoyed regular sex—maybe more. He could make her come endless times, until she was throbbing and restless, until she had to beg him to come inside her.

God, she loved it.

Two weeks wasn't a long time, but she felt incredibly close to Blake. She trusted him with her body—and hell, with her heart. She had dated her last boyfriend for months without feeling this level of intimacy. He certainly had never done *this* to her, lapping from the bottom to the top, lingering in a lazy circle around her clit, pressing in an instinctual rhythm until her hips took up the beat.

Before she could climax, Blake licked and sucked his way lower. His tongue slipped between her lips, sparking tendrils of need through her core.

"Oh, no," she moaned, lost to the sensations, shuddering on the edge.

"What is it, baby?" he murmured against her flesh. "Tell me what you want. Take what you need. I'm not going to stop. However long it takes."

She fisted his hair and guided his mouth to her clit. He sucked her, using his lips and tongue to drive her higher and further until she was taut, stretched out, and ready to burst.

It was the touch of his fingers to her inner lips that pushed her over, a tickle combined with the harsh pleasure at her clit, and she came in a sunburst that belied the heavy shadows surrounding them.

Slowly coming down, she blinked up at the ceiling, feeling energized. "Now I'm well and truly awake."

"Shit," he said, sounding dismayed.

"It's not a complaint, mister. That was amazing."

"Don't worry." He lowered his mouth to her sex, amusement and arousal warring in his voice. "I think we can wear you out all over again."

She would have smiled then, but his tongue curled and his fingers delved deep. Her thighs drew up tight, and she came again, smaller this time, intense, rolling waves. He didn't give her a reprieve, just set the flat of his tongue against her clit, which was at once too sensitive and exactly what she needed. She grew louder, her body writhing without her control, but each new orgasm sent her farther into the sex-drugged space.

When her body shuddered in one final orgasm, he knelt between her legs. She noticed distantly that his hands were shaking as he put on the condom, as he angled his cock at her slippery cunt and pushed inside. It was all wonderful but never more than that moment, when she felt so full and watched an expression of bliss soothe his tortured face.

On the one side, his skin was smooth, aside from the ruggedness and bristle of an active, healthy man. The flesh on the other side had once been burned, ravaged by fire and war, now covered with scar tissue.

It hurt to see, but only because she ached for him, for the pain he felt then, for the pain he felt *now*. It kept him locked up in his immaculate house instead of out in the world.

He was beautiful.

In the moonlight, the jagged landscape of his scars was more pronounced. But it was his slack jaw that she admired, his glazed eyes. The signs of his ecstasy brought on by her body. As if he were a god, she offered herself up to him, but it wasn't a sacrifice to feel the heavy weight of his muscles, the thick pulse of his cock, the tender press of his lips against her when he bent to drop a kiss. He thrust inside her, faster and harder, pushing them onward in a sea of molten pleasure.

"Fuck," he muttered. "I can't—I can't—"

"Don't hold back." Then she repeated his earlier words. "Take what you need."

That seemed to release him.

He picked up speed, slamming inside her so

hard it took her breath away. He pressed his lips to hers, moving his tongue to the same rhythm as his hips. He invaded her at both places, her mouth and her sex, and held her down in all the rest, but she wouldn't have moved for the world. She longed for him to take her, to use her.

Anything she could do to bring him pleasure.

Anything to bring him peace.

His hips lost their steady motion, jerking up against her like waves on a cliff, crashing until he let out a hoarse shout and held still for his climax. Long moments spent in the most intimate way a woman can hold a man, with her secret muscles, drawing out his come.

He did not collapse on top of her. Very carefully, gingerly, he pulled out.

She whimpered slightly at the loss.

He stroked her thigh. "I'll be right back. Have to take care of this."

He disappeared into the bathroom to dispose of the condom. The water ran in a quiet rush. She stared at the glowing yellow edges of the door, resolved to wait until he got back into bed. There were problems they hadn't quite discussed, ones without a quick resolution—the fact that she was still a broke college student, for one thing. The fact that he was at least fifteen years older than her, well established and wealthy. No single conversation would resolve those issues. Wasn't it better to try, though? To talk about them? To make him understand that she, at least, was willing to be with him no matter the cost.

But his clever tongue and determination had done their job, and she was too exhausted to last. Beneath the shadow of defeat, she drifted off to sleep.

BLAKE

BLAKE RETURNED TO the bed, admiring the smooth cheek and dark eyelashes of his lover. Her brown hair looked like spun gold in the night, her skin pale as the moon. His gaze roamed lower, to the sweep of her neck and below. The sheet bared one breast—gorgeous and round, topped with a dusky nipple. He hadn't paid enough attention to her breasts this time, but then he always felt like that. He wanted to lick and suck every part of her body and then do it again.

He didn't fool himself about the ever-present tinge of desperation, as if he needed to hurry, as if she'd slip through his fingers like sand in the wind. He had realistic expectations.

He was ugly as sin. She was the most beautiful

woman he'd ever seen.

It was only a matter of time before she never came back.

Though it wasn't just his looks. They were a symptom of the root problem. Regular people could lock away their wounds and their weaknesses. Blake's hung like a sign on a storefront. A label on a map. *Here Be Dragons.* Everyone heeded the warning.

No one had ventured near him—until Erin.

He was fundamentally changed after his tour. Not just the explosion, although that had messed him up but good. For those long months overseas, he'd turned into something subhuman. Something with instincts, with power—something animal.

The things he'd seen still haunted him. He didn't much feel like being around people at all, and when they recoiled from him in fear it didn't help matters.

Maybe they *should* be afraid of him. Maybe the explosion had truly changed him, honed and sharpened him into something only useful for fighting—not living.

He'd existed in a world of darkness and palpable hellfire since the explosion and his return. So much for a life in the public spotlight. The well-planned career on a political stage was ruined. His parents were disappointed.

His fiancée had been disappointed too, until she'd left.

Hell, he was getting maudlin. He tried not to do that, especially when Erin was around. She had changed all that. He wasn't fixed—not even close. Hope was a small blade of green poking up from the hard, cracked earth.

As she'd said, he was well and truly awake now. If he stayed in bed with her, he'd only keep her up with his restlessness. With his relentless arousal.

Despite his pensive mood, his dick was ready for round two—or was it three or four? A steady state around her. He couldn't keep badgering her like this. He may live like a hermit these days, working at odd hours and all through the night, but she had to leave early in the morning.

Treading quietly, he slipped out of the bedroom to his study across the hall. The answering machine blinked red like it had all afternoon, but he ignored it. He didn't want to talk to anyone. Instead he flipped the screen up on his laptop, suffusing the room with a dim blue light that comforted him. Here he was in his element. Here he was treated as an equal.

There were six new emails today, each several pages long, dense blocks of text he'd sift through, dissect, and debate. Four from professors and politicos in the U.S., one abroad, and the last from a Jain monk in India. Well, the man's assistant, technically, since he didn't use a computer or even prepare his own food. The topics varied from domestic politics, global events, human rights, anything they could discuss passionately and endlessly, spinning his intellectual wheels in the rut of rhetoric. A network he'd built up over his years as a young, ambitious soldier with his eye on public office, never realizing he would one day need them as his sole link to humanity.

He lost himself in the words. Only here, he didn't have to be himself. The subjects tested him intellectually, but he didn't have to think about his own life and the lack of it. Not about Erin and when she might realize what a loser she'd hooked up with.

Not how he'd feel when she walked away.

Hours slipped away with only the clean, crisp notes of logical arguments, falling one after the other in a melody he could play in his sleep.

"You're awake."

He looked up to see Erin standing in the

doorway. Her arms were crossed, her slender body leaning back just inside the doorframe. He wondered how long she had been there.

"Oh man, I'm sorry." He stood up quickly, and pain shot down his neck. Partly it was the position he'd been in, but his neck had been stiff ever since the explosion. Months of physical therapy and rehabilitation visits had only helped so much. The explosion had damaged more than his skin. "I didn't realize how long it'd been."

She shrugged, wandering closer. "It's okay. You can work whenever you want."

Like a beacon, her presence shone light on things better left dark. She brushed her fingers over a dusty pile of papers. He'd told her to skip this room on her first visit here, and despite everything that had happened between them, he'd never changed that. Her first time in this room, the one place he'd felt alive in those dim hours, and her presence somehow felt more intimate than the sex they'd shared.

"Let's go back in the bedroom." His voice came out hoarse. "I can think of something better to do."

"Not sleep, though, I guess." Something seemed different about her, a diffidence. A chill in the air between them. She ran her fingers along his desk and gently blew the dust off her finger. "If I didn't know any better, I'd think you were hiding something from me."

He wasn't, not like she meant, so why did he suddenly feel guilty? Because she didn't know the extent of his injuries and PTSD. Because she didn't know how much he longed for her. Because she didn't know how lost he was when not anchored to her. He couldn't divulge any of that without losing part of himself—without losing her.

"Ask me anything you want to know," he said. His voice sounded raw, because that was how he felt. Exposed here, vulnerable. For her, yes.

She swiped a finger across the top of his glowing laptop—of course that one came away clean. One of the few things disturbed here. "Is there another woman in the picture?"

Shock mingled with relief as he laughed. "What? No."

"I mean, our relationship was pretty sudden. I'm not saying we have to be exclusive or that I expect that from you."

He spoke bluntly to put a stop to that. "There's no one else for me, Erin."

"Then why do always come in here when you

think I'm asleep? I know you already work in here all day. When do you rest?"

He opened his mouth to respond and then realized he didn't know the answer. She hadn't stayed over every night in the two weeks they'd been sleeping together, but dawn usually found him right in that leather swivel chair, eyes bleary from staring at the screen. He'd gone from being active in graduate school and in the military to...nothing. He still felt that drive, that ambition, but he had nowhere to put it, nowhere to go.

Seeming to assume he'd refused to answer, she wandered to a shelf piled high with books— academic journals that were probably years old, highlighted and dog-eared.

Her hand stilled over the answering machine. It blinked red up at her. She turned to him in question, asking if she should press it.

He shrugged. He had no idea who it was nor did he care, but if it would help ease her mind that there wasn't some other woman, some secret plot, then he'd rather she listened.

Instead she faced away, speaking to the door. "I didn't mean to snoop or...or accuse you of things. I never wanted to be that girl."

"They're reasonable questions. I *want* you to

ask them. No, I'm not with anyone. You. I want only you." And he didn't want her to be with anyone else either.

She made a small gasping sound, like a sob pulled up short.

"I'm so sorry," she breathed. "It's not that I don't trust you."

He waited, because it seemed like she might not trust him. There were a lot of reasons he was the wrong man for her, but not because he would betray her.

Her laugh was breathless. "Okay, I guess it does mean that. I just…have some trust issues. It's just that you're strong and secure, and I'm…well, I'm a train wreck, basically. I don't have enough money in my account to cover rent, and it's due in five days."

"I can help you with that."

"No. Absolutely not. That wasn't some kind of sly request for a sugar daddy. I don't want your money, especially now that we're sleeping together."

"It wouldn't be like that."

"That's exactly how it would be. Dirty and cheap."

He refrained from telling her that he would give her all his money. His house, his car. Every goddamn cent in his bank account—which would make her far from cheap. That probably wouldn't help his case any. The words *sugar daddy* made him swallow hard. Was that how they were together? It made him feel like he was taking advantage of her—even more so since he hadn't actually given her a cent since they first kissed.

"What if you moved in with me? You're sleeping here almost every night."

He already hated every time she left. Then she wouldn't have to pay rent at her apartment, which he knew from the address wasn't in a very safe part of town.

She spun to face him, her eyes glistening in the dark. Her lips trembled. "You mean that? No, it would be the same thing. I actually want… I need us to take this slow."

Slow? That was the opposite of how he felt about her. Every part of him wanted to claim her, to take her as his own so no other man could ferry her away when she went out into the world while he was trapped here.

"So I can sort out my life stuff, without worrying about…us."

"No problem," he said, achieving some level of casualness. "That's what we'll do."

If it killed him, that's what he'd do. Because

there was an *us*, whatever that meant, and he'd do anything to keep it that way. Even stand by while she struggled financially. Christ.

The goddamned red light was still blinking, mocking his inability to communicate with the outside world. Distracted, and maybe needing to prove something about his trustworthiness even if she wasn't ready to believe it, he pressed the button to play while she looked on.

"Hi, Blake, this is Jeremy. Jeremy Mosely, Dean of Social Sciences. You remember we spoke about the Associate Professor's position? I know you turned me down then, and we went ahead and hired some bigwig advisor from Washington to come down for the summer semester. But wouldn't you know, his guy got elected and now he's backing out of the contract. Can't change his mind and we've got a class without a professor. We'd love for you to reconsider…ah, who am I kidding? We're desperate at this point. It's only one class. Name your terms, Blake. You were always the best man for the job."

Jeremy rattled off some phone numbers, but Blake didn't move. Damn. He hadn't really wanted Erin to know about that. It would only serve to highlight his uselessness. His brokenness. The fact that he didn't have a job, beyond the occasional article in an esoteric professional journal or consulting on a grant application. Of course, the cat was out of the bag now, and if he tried to backtrack in any way, she would only look at it like he was hiding something.

A smile spread over her pretty face. "They want to hire you at the university? Associate Professor?" She laughed happily and launched herself at him, wrapping her arms around his neck. "That's amazing, Blake."

Shit. He hugged her back and then gently set her away. "Erin, it's not going to work out."

"But he said you could name your terms. You think you could get an office with a window in it?"

"I don't care about the office. I mean, there's not going to be an office."

Her head jerked back at his sharp tone.

He softened, pleading a little. "It's just not a good time."

She looked around the small cluttered space as if she were seeing it for the first time. After a long moment, she said quietly, "I see."

Goddamn her, she probably did see. She saw the thick walls that separated him from the rest of the world, shielding him from their sight. And then what? Would she walk out and never return?

Would he wish that she had, knowing some stronger, more functional man could better care for her? He couldn't let that happen.

The inevitability washed over him, and he shut his eyes against the deluge. She wanted to *go slow* so she could figure out her life; the truth was he needed to do his own figuring out. Truth was he needed to do this for himself. How long could he remain in hibernation before he withered away to nothing?

His throat constricted, but he managed to say with no small amount of futility, "I'll talk to him tomorrow. If the position is still open, I'll take it."

CHAPTER FIVE

ERIN

A SENSE OF rightness filled Erin as she ducked into the social sciences building. She'd been flush with anticipation all through her morning classes, knowing she would get to see Blake at lunchtime.

She had been busy working for a maid service that sent her to fancy homes around the city. Between the new job and studying, she was exhausted. That didn't stop her from driving to Blake's house almost every evening.

They were consigned to the night, with take-out and a movie downstairs. They'd tear open the fortune cookies, adding "in bed" to whatever it gave them for the future. *Soon life will become more interesting...in bed.* And then Blake would set about proving it true in a languorous lovemaking session in his bedroom until the sun streamed between his blinds. Blake had joked that he was a gargoyle, turned to stone at sunrise.

A not-so-subtle reference to the scars marring his handsome face.

This was different. Blake had accepted a position as a temporary adjunct professor with the university. Now she would get to see him in the daytime.

She balanced two lattes from the vendor outside, slipping through the heavy crowd of students exiting the lecture rooms. A few banded together in small lines in front of the closed office doors. Office hours most commonly ran during the middle of the day between the usual blocks of class times. They began the week before classes started, to allow students to meet their new professors.

In Erin's case, she had gone to see her advisor, who she already knew from previous years. He was smart and unassuming, so she liked him. He'd given her feedback on her preliminary ideas for the final research paper. She would incorporate his critique into her outline over the next few days, and he would sign off on it when school began.

She had one more stop to make before she left campus.

Professor Morris. The name made her flush with sexual heat. Probably because she'd called him that when he went down on her last night.

His position was temporary, but the letters were freshly engraved on the frosted glass of his office door. They must be hopeful he'd stick around beyond the summer semester.

Voices came from inside. Damn. Someone had beat her to him. Ah well, better that way. Then he could spend the rest of his office time with her. Oh, she knew he had a job to do. Amusing Erin Rodriguez wasn't why the university had begged him to be an adjunct professor. But it was the first week of classes; how many questions could they have?

Someone jostled her in the hallway, and scalding coffee spilled onto her hand.

"Ouch," she muttered.

A shadow moved in the office, then another. So there were a few students in there, chatting up the new professor to get in his good graces. With a start, she realized that must be exactly how she looked, coming to bribe him with a coffee. A blush heated her cheeks far more than the hot liquid could. If only they knew what she *really* did for him.

But no one could know.

They had agreed not to tell anyone. More accurately, she had talked him out of disclosing their prior relationship. The position would be toast if the university knew he had a sexual relationship with a student, even if she wasn't *his* student. It was an ethical black mark, but no way was she letting him get out of his return to society.

Nor would she allow their relationship to jeopardize her graduation.

One short semester. Only six weeks and they'd both be free. They could have a relationship out in the open. Maybe she would actually move in with him, once she had a job that could pay for her share of the bills. Bliss.

The hallway thinned to the occasional straggler.

Finally the office door opened, and two girls tumbled out, a flurry of tiny tank tops and scrunchies, the kind of adorable, I-just-threw-this-on look that Erin always envied. They barely spared her a glance, but some sense of propriety held her back from rushing inside before the door swung shut. No need to draw attention to her double-fisted coffee routine.

Acting casual, she hitched her backpack on her shoulder and reached for the latch on the door. With her back turned, she heard them speak.

"Did you see his face?" one of them said, giggling.

"I couldn't stop looking, and *not* in a good way," the other replied.

Erin froze. She held the door handle, but she was stunned by their awful words. They weren't making any effort to be quiet, despite the fact that they'd only made it two feet away. She wasn't sure if Blake could hear them from inside, but if she opened the door right now, he definitely would.

The first girl sighed. "Yeah, but when he turned around…damn, I didn't mind looking then. He can write on the blackboard as long as he wants."

"Mm-hmm," the other agreed. "That was a fine piece of ass, no doubt. As long as he faces the other direction, I could stare at him all day."

They continued down the hallway as anger bubbled up inside her. She'd always considered herself a passable feminist; certainly outright objectification or meanness bothered her. But here it was directed at not only a man, but the man she cared about. The man she loved.

Swallowing hard, she pushed inside.

"Hey, Professor. You have a minute?"

Blake looked up from his desk and smiled. "For you, always."

She looked at him with fresh eyes, trying to imagine him as a professor she'd come to meet, as if she were a regular student instead of his maid. One half of his face was handsome, beautiful even. The other was matted with heavy burn scars from the top of his lip to his temple. His eye was still functional, but the shape didn't match the other side, giving him a mismatched appearance.

She liked everything about the way he looked. The bravery of his military service, the bravery he showed going out into the world despite how people judged him. How precious it was that he'd lived, that he was with her.

Suffused with sudden emotion, she shoved the coffees onto a cluttered file cabinet and launched her arms around his neck. He caught her with an *oomph* but soon after tightened his embrace into a hug.

"What's gotten into you?" he asked, laughing softly.

I'm so proud of you. But she didn't want to bring it up if he hadn't heard those girls. He seemed in good spirits. Instead she said, "Missed you."

"You saw me last night," he reminded her.

She pulled back, smiling slyly. "And again this morning."

His eyes darkened, and she felt him thickening against her belly. He was so quick to arousal, always ready for more.

Holding his gaze, she slid her hand down. His stomach was taut beneath the button-down and undershirt she'd watched him don this morning. Her fingers crossed the ridge of his belt like it was the damned Rubicon, the point of no return. They were in his office, but they were alone…and damn it, she felt the need to please him. To pleasure him after those ridiculous girls had sullied him, whether he knew it or not. She found his erection, thick and pulsing.

He bucked into her hand, groaning. "Erin. Oh fuck, *Erin*."

She loved her name on his lips.

"Yes?" she asked innocently. "Is something wrong?"

He gasped out something she couldn't understand. It didn't matter. His body told her what she needed to know: the heat beneath her palm, the shudder of his thighs beneath the smooth slacks. The arousal that fine wool and linen did little to conceal. He needed this as much as she did. God, he looked good in a suit. She wouldn't have blamed those girls for their gawking if they hadn't been so cruel about his scars.

She sank to her knees, pushing him gently against the wall. Their bodies blocked the door; no one would be able to walk in and see them. But someone could try, and what would their excuse be for blocking the way? Even worse, if someone outside were very near and very quiet, they might be able to hear the ragged breaths wrenched from Blake's throat, the rasp of his zipper as she tugged it down, the low groan as she pulled him out, skin to skin.

The risk excited her. So different from the safe circle of his bedroom. It felt, somehow, like a declaration. A statement of intent. *He's mine.*

He was heavy in her hand, a weight she'd expect from a man who hadn't been laid in months. Instead he was like this every time. Large enough to fill her palm, her sex...her mouth. A wicked smile tilted her lips.

His nostrils flared, higher on the right side than the left. "God, Erin. What are you doing to me?"

"Should I stop, Professor Morris?"

BLAKE

SHOULD SHE STOP? *No, don't stop, ever.*

Wait. Blake forced the lust fever back, allowed

his mind to clear and really think about what they were doing. She looked so beautiful there, with her lips a full, pouty pink and her dark eyes sultry with arousal, that he almost couldn't control himself, almost couldn't stop. But she deserved better than being on her knees in this dusty office where someone might walk in. She deserved a lot better than him, but now that he had her, he didn't plan on giving her up anytime soon.

He should be able to control himself better when he was so well practiced in denial, but damn it, he wanted those pink lips on him, he wanted her sweet, warm heat, but he wanted so much more. Her moans, her pleasure.

"Are you sure we should be doing this here?" His voice came out hoarse, belying any consideration implied in his words. He wanted this so fucking bad.

She squeezed gently, making his hips jerk. She smiled, pleased with her power. "If you tell me to stop, I will."

Ah, hell. So beautiful. He squeezed his eyes shut against the sight, but he couldn't last for long that way, feeling the brush of her breath against his exposed cock.

"Erin."

"Yes, Professor?"

He narrowed his eyes, feeling on the verge of some discovery, on the edge of the cliff and he would jump just to be with her.

"You like this." Surprise filled his voice. Surprise and wonder.

A small smile curved her lips, though she didn't answer.

"The idea that someone might walk in on us. It turns you on. It excites you."

Her cheeks darkened with a blush. She kept her eyes trained on his cock as her hands took up a steady stroke. He wouldn't be distracted.

"Stand up then," he rasped. "Let me take care of you."

She shook her head, slow and coy. God, she turned him on. She only had to look at him, to smile, and he was revved up, ready to burst. But when she was like this, seductive, empowered, he wanted to fall at her feet.

But that wasn't what she wanted.

"And maybe the power, too," he mused. "You like me being in control. The role-play."

"Well, you are a professor."

"And you're a student. A naughty one."

She laughed. "Am I?"

Oh yes. For her, he would play any game, pay any price, and this was no hardship at all.

He knelt in front of her, taking her face in his hands and kissing her forehead gently. "That's right. Coming into a professor's office and taking out his cock. Do you do that for all your teachers?"

She blushed fiercely, eyes downcast. "No, sir."

"Only me, then? This is your first time holding a professor's cock in your hand?"

"Oh God," she moaned. Then she righted herself. "Yes, sir."

Fuck, when she called him sir, it made him lose his mind. "Do you think that was a wise move? I must say, you don't seem to know what to do with it next."

She startled at his words, jerking her hand on him. Too much, too fast—he'd blow before the game had finished.

"No, that won't do at all." He tsked. "Looks like I'll have to teach you to do this as well. I hope you can be a better student now than you are in class."

"Oh, I will." Her eyes danced with arousal and latent humor. Comfortable with each other, she and Blake kept to their roles, the pleasure well worth the charade, but beneath that they communicated with a sly glance and familiar caress.

"You'll be a good girl for me," he murmured.

"Yes," she begged, and he was lost, her willing slave in the form of a harsh taskmaster, wanting to please her in any way, any form, and illicit role-play was on order.

Slowly he stood up, running the pad of his thumb along her plush lower lip. "Then let's put this mouth to better use."

BLAKE

A GLISTENING DROP of precum formed on the tip of his cock, giving lie to the sternness he presented. She wasn't complaining, though. He filled out his role so well, both the lovely embarrassing words and the heft in her hand. Her mouth watered to taste him, but the tease was too fun to give up early.

"I'm so upset about getting a B, Professor Morris. I'm really an A-plus kind of student." Of course it was all a game. This wasn't reality; it was a sex world, a pretend place of security and wholeness.

She continued, "Is there anything I can do to convince you? I'm really quite diligent when I put my mind to the task."

His eyes were slits, his upper lip lifted in a

snarl of arousal. It was scary, and that excited her. She wasn't frightened of him. His expression was feral because his lust was wild. Underneath, the man was gentle. Exceedingly kind. In fact, she'd thought he wouldn't play along. That he wouldn't be comfortable playing the role she'd cast him into. But she should have known better than to doubt him. He had never disappointed her yet.

"I'm sure I can think of some extra credit work for you to do." His hand pressed gently behind her neck, urging her forward, closer, until she could smell the faint salty musk.

"I don't know what you want me to do," she said breathlessly, wanting him to use those dirty words she so enjoyed.

He brought his thumb to her lips, rubbing across them in a way that heightened every nerve in her body. "A good student must apply herself," he said, his voice gravelly and thick with need. "Do you understand what I'm saying?"

"Won't you give me instructions?" she whispered.

"Lick it. Here." Guiding himself with one hand, he placed the soft, slippery skin at the tip against her lips. Tentatively, she licked. Outwardly she played the innocent, but inside she reveled in the salty-sex flavor of his passion.

Obliging him and taking it farther, she licked the tender slit again and again. His breath hitched sweetly at each slide of her tongue, but soon he moved on, directing her to lick and suck all over the broad head of his cock, down the underside.

He tapped her bottom lip. "Open."

She dutifully opened her mouth. He angled his cock inside, thrusting gently as she grew accustomed to his girth. He was too large to move in her mouth quickly. She would inevitably gag, and he didn't like that. It didn't matter to her, but he minded any hint of her discomfort.

In steady pulses, he rocked against her face, climbing closer to orgasm. She could tell by the heavy breaths, the tightening of his fist in her hair. When she thought he would explode in her mouth, he pushed her back. In seconds she was up against the wall where he had been, her jeans yanked down and his mouth pressed to her core.

Gasping, he pulled away only long enough to say, "Couldn't wait anymore."

Then his mouth was back at her folds, licking and sucking. Pleasure coursed through her, sharp and sweet. Her hips bucked just like his, only more eager now that she was primed. She couldn't help it; she rocked against the lovely pressure, humping his face, though the low groans told her he didn't mind much.

Sensation raced over her skin, heightened by her eagerness all day, her anger at those girls, her love for this man. She climbed a peak, propelled by clever fingers and a wicked tongue. Frantic sounds escaped her, unwilling to be held back even at the expense of discovery. She rocked and shuddered, and with the smooth, slick curl of his tongue against her clit, found completion in a soft rush and sated sigh.

He turned her around, bending her over the file cabinet. She grasped the sides, the metal cool and slick beneath her sweaty palms. She heard the condom wrapper tear, felt him nudge her from behind, felt her slick, swollen flesh part for the broad head of his cock. He didn't waste time; as if his restraint had eroded, he pushed inside, smooth and fast. She gasped at the feeling of being full—too full, a pleasurable hum stretching into an ache deep inside. That small pain was the sweetest, a signal of his loss of control, a sign of his lust. She clenched her muscles, reveling in the low groan pulled from him. He set up a hard, swift rhythm, pulling almost all the way out before plunging to the hilt. She could only hold on, only cling to the hard metal surface with her mouth open in a silent cry until he froze and dug into her hips and throbbed inside her as he came.

For a moment, he curved his strong body over hers in repose and possession. His breath was harsh against the back of her neck, mingling with hers in the cool, dusty air. All too soon, he pulled out—more gently now, gingerly even.

She started to stand, but he pressed her lower back to keep her still.

"Let me clean you." His voice was rough, an audible remnant of the passion they'd just shared. He tore a paper towel from the roll on a bookcase.

She squirmed at the rasp of paper on her tender flesh. She reached back to take it from him, but he stayed her hand.

"Let me," he repeated.

Biting her lip, she remained still for his touch.

"It's too bright in here," she whispered. He could see every part of her this way. Bent over, she was exposed. Her cunt, her asshole—all of it on display. The corner of the cabinet was cutting into her belly now, more noticeable without the haze of arousal.

He trailed a finger through her inner lips up through the crease in her ass, wringing a shudder from her. "You're beautiful here. Everywhere."

It pained her that he meant it as a contrast to him, but she didn't know how to comfort him without raising the issue herself. A kind word could turn the knife already inside him if she wasn't careful. In the end, he solved the problem by bringing it up himself.

"You didn't have to do it," he said.

"Do what?"

"Have sex in my office because those girls insulted me."

He spoke so flatly, without emotion, such a contrast to the warm joy that had filled his voice just seconds before that she felt the loss reverberate in her heart. So he'd heard them. And he'd known all along what had driven her—but he would interpret that as pity, not…well, what was it? Kindness? Love? She wanted him to be happy, not to worry, but the world would always judge him, would always mock and belittle him for the scars he'd earned protecting it.

She understood then why he kept her bent over for his admission. It was the veil of confession, distance and darkness allowing the words to come out. The fact that he'd admitted it at all cut her to the quick. He'd been willing to accept the sex he didn't believe he deserved, but he would release her of any further obligation.

She turned, ignoring his damned divide, and framed his face in her hands. Both sides, one

BEAUTY AND THE PROFESSOR

chiseled jaw gently bristled with hair, the other wavy and lacking in hair. Surprise flickered in his deep brown eyes.

"Damn you," she said. "I had sex with you because I wanted to. Because I wanted *you*, and unless you want an argument on your hands, you damn well better not forget it."

He blinked, taken aback. Well, she was too. A little shell-shocked, a little desperate. In some ways, they were close, intimate. Certainly the sex was amazing. But in other ways, she couldn't break through. His scars were just the surface. He still suffered nightmares for what had happened there. He would always be chained by a past she couldn't unlock.

"Just let me in," she whispered, a breath away from his lips.

His eyes searched hers. "All of me, Erin. You already have all of me."

Even while the sweet words sent joy through her heart, sadness weighed her down. This was all he could give her, he meant. And it would have to be enough, for now.

The sound of a friendly shout from down the hall pulled her attention to the present, the physical. She quickly arranged her clothes back into place. A rueful smile curved Blake's lips as he did the same and tossed the paper towel into the trash.

She raised an eyebrow. "Do you always keep that handy for sex?"

He grinned, which looked charmingly crooked. In reality, it was the scars that tugged one side of his mouth, but that lopsided smile never failed to tighten her chest.

"Just cleaning up," he said, resting on the edge of his desk. "It's dusty in these offices."

"I think it's all that intellect," she teased. "Can't help but get a little full of yourselves."

"Ah, but you're the ones with the fresh ideas. We had our chance to change the world. Now it's your turn."

"You talk like you're so old."

"I am so old."

He had fifteen years on her, but she was positive he could run five miles—and a lot faster than she could. His body was in ridiculous shape. "You keep up pretty well."

His huff of laughter placated her. One day he would believe in them as much as she did. Until then…well, until then she would enjoy every second they spent together.

She plucked the roll of paper towels from beside him and replaced it on the bookshelf.

While there, she scanned the older texts that she imagined had been here before. One shelf was noticeably brighter than the others—recently cleaned, no doubt—and contained a few books she recognized from his house.

The other half had the composition notebooks he was always scribbling his ideas in, new and stacked up. He would write something brilliant, an offhand thought that she would consider from every angle before confirming it was correct.

His mind was a treasure trove, and his body, she was finding, was the map. She could follow the sleek lines, traverse the hard-packed muscles and salty earth and learn him inch by inch, but she'd be no closer to her goal. Great sex would never be enough for her. She wanted *him*.

CHAPTER SIX

ERIN

FOOTSTEPS CAME FROM outside the door, rapidly approaching. Another student to see Blake? She wasn't sure, but she had taken up enough of his time.

"I'll get going," she said with a small smile.

He groaned. "It's going to kill me being so close to you, knowing you're on the same campus, maybe even in the same building, but not able to touch you."

She grinned. "Maybe I can visit you in office hours. Not too often, mind you, but I'm sure you have a few more lessons to teach me."

He laughed, and she would have laughed with him, except she was too stunned by the sight of him happy with abandon. So distracted that she only barely registered the turning of the office doorknob.

The door slammed open, rattling the bookshelf and sending dust into the air. She coughed, taking in the woman who stood in the doorway. Even if another student had come, Erin would have expected her to wait outside, as she had done, or at least to knock. But now she saw this was no student. The woman was older, dressed in a sleek suit jacket and pencil skirt. Her hair was a coppery red, pale enough to border on strawberry blonde. Her skin had the translucence of a natural redhead peppered with freckles.

And Erin knew her.

"Professor Jenkins," she said in surprise.

Professor Jenkins turned to her. "Ms. Rodriguez. What are you doing here?"

God, what *was* she doing here? Her fingers flipping through Blake's personal notebook stash. Her clothes—thankfully back in place but still rumpled.

"Cleaning," she said.

Professor Jenkins blinked once, then twice. She spoke to Blake. "You have a maid for your office?"

Admittedly it was a bit strange, considering the room was smaller than the average bedroom. But Blake was smart—he caught on quickly. Benefit of sleeping with a Rhodes scholar, she supposed.

"Erin cleans my house," he answered. "I asked

her to come by today. The office was a mess when I got here."

Hah! And he didn't even technically lie.

Professor Jenkins's cool green eyes gave Erin a quick appraisal. Disheveled hair from their lovemaking, plain jeans, and a T-shirt—standard fare for a student, but there were no designer labels here. Just as fast, the woman lost interest in her, her expression making Erin's lack of appeal clear.

The maid. The hired help. Nobody at all.

Once again, she was dismissed for what she did to pay the bills. Erin was used to it among the other students at the private university. No one was gauche enough to say anything about it. She couldn't afford the thirty-dollar shots of sake or bottles of champagne they liked to order. Eventually she'd found different friends. Other scholarship kids or ones who had the money but didn't flaunt it. But Erin never forgot how out of place she'd felt, how little.

Maybe she'd been naïve, but she'd expected more from a professor. Erin was a hard worker, someone who paid her bills on time, in full. But in this private university, where her tuition was covered half on scholarship and half on loans, she was just a charity case.

Professor Jenkins turned to Blake. "Well, then," she said brightly. "I'm glad you're taking your new position here seriously."

Before Erin could process the sweet, almost personal tone, the woman stepped closer to Blake. The office was small, so perhaps the close quarters could be explained that way. But it didn't feel like it. As if dismissing Erin from sight and from mind, as if Erin were as deaf and dumb as the file cabinet, the woman spoke intimately.

"Lord knows I tried to get you to come back here after the accident."

"It had been a week," he said dryly.

"Well, the important thing is that you're here now, and things can go back to the way they were. I have to admit, I've missed you, Blake."

Erin stared, giving up any pretense that she was cleaning, that she wasn't watching. She finally put her finger on what she sensed from Professor Jenkins: possession. It was the same way Erin looked at Blake, like she knew him so well, like she owned some part of him.

If she'd had her doubts, the dark expression on Blake's face sealed the deal. He and Professor Jenkins had definitely been lovers, she just knew it.

Maybe more, maybe committed.

Which shouldn't matter but somehow did. Erin trusted Blake, and they were together now. He wasn't about to cheat on her the second her back was turned...or when she was right there in the room. Then again they hadn't made any commitments.

And they weren't allowed to tell anyone they were together. Though she tried so hard not to think about it...it made her feel like a dirty little secret.

"That was a long time ago, Melinda," he said softly.

She hesitated, as if she wasn't expecting that, then laughed. "We were both young and stupid then. Things have changed."

He shook his head. His smile was more of a grimace. "Not that much."

A small sound escaped Erin.

Professor Jenkins looked over, as if just noticing she was still here. "Maybe you can finish up here another time," she told Erin, her voice hard. "I need to have a private talk with Dr. Morris."

"No, Melinda," he said, sliding past her to open the door. "We don't need to have a private talk, and she doesn't have to go."

He was going to tell her, Erin realized. Whether he said the words or not, he'd give it away. And somehow she knew that Melinda Jenkins was vindictive enough to use it against him…and her. He needed this job to return to the world, to become part of it again. She needed to complete her final research paper and get it approved by the board.

"No, that's okay," she said quickly. "I have a class soon anyway. I'll just go."

Blake frowned, clearly ready to countermand her, so she grabbed her backpack and stumbled out the door before he could stop her. Melinda's shrill laugh followed her down the hallway. More words about making up for lost time.

Erin sped up, the tiles blurring under her feet and tears glazing her eyes.

Damn it.

She just felt so small and unimportant, even though she didn't have a reason to be, not really. Blake hadn't done anything wrong, and neither had Professor Jenkins. Erin was the third wheel, the young, poor college student who had seduced him.

When was the last time he'd seen another woman before he and Erin had hooked up? And she had paraded around his house twice a week, fawning over him with a ridiculous crush. No wonder he'd had sex with her. Any man would have.

That didn't mean he'd want to continue. It didn't mean he should.

Maybe he was better off with someone like Melinda. She could help establish him in the real world better with his colleagues at the university. She had the financial means to match him, the right image to stand beside him. He wouldn't have to hide his relationship with her. Would they also have noontime sex in his office?

It made Erin want to throw something.

Her phone vibrated from the front pocket of her backpack.

She pulled it out to see her mother's smiling face on the small, dim screen. Her stomach dropped. With a lingering glance at Blake's office door, she pushed through the doors leading outside, blinking as the sun blinded her.

"Hey, Mom."

"Are you okay?" The worry in her mother's voice made guilt pool in her belly. She usually called once a week, sometimes more. But ever since she'd started seeing Blake, it had gotten harder to talk to her mother and still keep her secret.

"Of course I'm fine."

"I know you're busy, honey. I just worry."

She knew exactly the moment when her mother had lost all faith in Erin's ability to judge people or make it on her own. Erin knew because she doubted herself too.

A change of subject was in order. "School's starting next week. One more semester."

She heard the smile in her mother's voice. "I'm thrilled for you, sweetie. You deserve this. What are you doing now, working?"

"No, I'm on campus." *Where I just got done having sex with a professor.* That would not ease her mother's worries. Pointing out that it was a relationship would only make things worse, not better. And now that Erin had time to reflect, she realized how impulsive she had been to do so. A very bad idea with a thankfully happy ending.

It was just…she'd never had much opportunity to be spontaneous and silly. She worked, she went to school. She wasn't complaining about it. Her mom had it harder than anyone, after all. But for the first time in her years at the university, Erin had felt young.

"I met with my advisor this morning." At least that much was true. Her visit to campus hadn't been solely a booty call. "We went over some of the requirements for my research paper. I'm going to work on my outline tonight."

"I'm sure you'll do great, sweetie."

Erin winced. Such faith, and here she was trying to have fun. This wasn't a game. "How are you, Mom? Work going okay?"

"Oh, you know. Work's work."

She sensed the hesitation. "Something's wrong. Tell me."

Her mother laughed. "I never could hide much from you. Just my knees acting up."

"You need to go to the—"

"To the doctor. I went. He wants me to have surgery."

Erin stopped in her tracks. The crowd of people sluiced around her as she stood in the middle of the sidewalk. If her mom had actually visited the doctor without being cajoled and forced into it, she must be in a lot of pain. "Surgery?"

"It doesn't matter. You know I can't afford it."

"They don't have any sort of programs or something, for low-income patients? A payment program?"

"I don't know, but I couldn't do it anyway. The surgery will make it so I can't work for weeks. Maybe even months. I can't take off work that long."

Erin closed her eyes. "Mom, if he says you need the surgery, we'll find a way."

"No, I'll figure it out, Erin. You don't worry about me. Focus on school."

Focus on school, and not an illicit relationship with a man way out of her league. Yeah, that was a fair request. Only she wasn't sure she could actually follow it. Leave Blake? Chills raced through her body. Wrong, all wrong.

"I will, mom. One more semester."

"One more semester and you'll never have to clean houses for a living. You'll never have to deal with this kind of problem, of not being able to afford your surgery or take time off to have it. That's all I want for you, honey. All I've ever wanted for you."

Her heart squeezed. "I know."

"That's my girl. You and me against the world," she said, as she always had since Erin was a kid. It was a secret club with just two members.

At one time it had been a comfort.

Her mother's goodbyes were happy and heart-felt as they hung up, but Erin felt stricken. Did it really come down to choosing between school and Blake? After all, when she eventually had a career, she'd have to juggle them, so she might as well learn to do it now.

She smiled without any humor. Blake might take the decision out of her hands. He might decide to rekindle what he had with Professor Jenkins.

Then Erin's problems would go away…

Ah, but they wouldn't. She loved him, simple as that. And it superseded so much. She wasn't willing to sacrifice her degree for that love, or her future, but she'd give up her pride. It wasn't worth much anyway.

BLAKE

A LOW GROWL emanated from Blake as he watched Erin leave the office. Their sexual encounter had been mind-blowing, more than he'd ever expected or hoped for, so much that his usual sense of foreboding had abandoned him completely, but it had all come crashing down.

Because of Melinda.

She was still here, coming up behind him, giving that trill laugh he'd once thought endearing. Fuck, he should have handled that better. Should have handled *her* better.

He'd been so damned surprised. Bowled over by the orgasm with Erin, by the shock of seeing Melinda after so long. And her innuendo that thcy might rekindle their relationship. Shit. No way in hell, and he'd been ready to tell her that.

He'd been ready to throw the position away. What did he need this job for anyway? He had already turned it down once. It wasn't worth upsetting Erin, and it sure as hell wasn't worth losing her. So he'd been about to tell Melinda exactly who Erin was, but maybe it was best that she'd interrupted him.

Erin was more than his lover; she'd been his ray of light in a dank, dark place. He wasn't even sure she knew how much he had relied on her presence, looked forward to her visits.

If he told her, she might run.

Hell, he thought with a sinking feeling, she'd already run. Down the hallway might as well be to the moon for all he could talk to her now, with Melinda breathing down his neck and a meeting with the dean in twenty minutes.

The students outside his office sounded like a herd of elephants, their voices augmenting one another and bouncing off the white-bright walls until his head pounded. His palms were sweaty, his heartbeat erratic, and it wasn't just the great sex or awkward encounter. He thought he was over these damn flashbacks, but it turned out he'd been avoiding them, staying home where no one ever came. Now he was immersed in people and drowning, suffocating.

Melinda propped a hip on the edge of his desk. "I think that girl might have a little crush on you. Fire her before she gets the wrong idea. Did you see the way she looked at you?"

Jesus, he needed to end this. "Probably the way everyone looks at me. Like my face was blown up and then sewn back together, which is exactly what happened."

"No, she looked at you the way they used to look at you. You were the handsomest man on campus then. And when you wore your uniform? None of the girls could keep their eyes off you back then. I'm sure it feels good to have even one crush now."

"Stop," he said dryly. "You'll flatter me."

"Oh, don't tell me you're offended. If there's one thing we've had between us, it's honesty. Your face is not handsome anymore. But I can live with the scarring."

"Funny, that's not how I remember it."

Melinda gave him a small smile, a pout that he assumed was contrite. "You have to admit it was a lot to handle."

Long-buried frustration surfaced. "Which part, Melinda? Because I didn't ask you for a damn thing before you walked out my door for the last time."

His bandages hadn't even come off yet. "It just isn't going to work out between us," she'd said, but inside he'd heard, *you're hideous, you're disgusting.*

Over time his anger at her had dissipated, because he *was* hideous. He was disgusting. And he'd been stuck in that place for a full year, swinging back and forth between waking depression and haunting dreams of his time overseas, of a blast that had shredded his life to ugly, misshapen pieces.

Then one day, he'd woken up amid pizza boxes and soda cans and realized that if he were going to keep on living—and since he hadn't died yet, he supposed he was—then he could at least live cleanly. So he'd pulled up the local job board and posted a message. Erin had replied and… Ah, Erin.

She had been a shot of healing heat in a bleak winter. Slowly he had improved himself, each day becoming a little stronger, coming back into his old self when he hadn't thought it was possible.

Melinda circled the desk, coming to stand beside him. Some unknown curiosity had him letting her. Was anything left, any of the love and devotion he'd once felt for her? It seemed hard to believe he could have spent the rest of his life with her…when now he felt nothing. Like looking at a stranger smile at him, like feeling the cool back of her palm touch the unmarred side of his face, the part that was normal.

"I thought I was going to marry Blake Morris. *The* Blake Morris, with a whole future ahead of him, maybe even a run for Congress one day. You looked so different. It wasn't just your scars. You were angry, withdrawn. I didn't know how much of you was left."

He moved her hand from his face. "You didn't stick around to find out."

"I freaked out. You can forgive a girl for that, can't you?"

"We're done, Melinda. You made that clear once."

"I was young," she said softly. "I thought appearances mattered."

He laughed, the sound bitter and sharp as razors. She was only a year younger than him, and if he wasn't mistaken, her dress suit was still designer. Her shoes probably cost five hundred dollars. "And I suppose now you're interested in what's on the inside, right? Or is it just my bank account you want back?"

She jerked her head back as if slapped. "That was low, Blake."

"Maybe." He sighed. "Yeah, it was. I shouldn't have said that. But this ends right here. I don't want you to come to my office unless you have school business to discuss."

A smile curved her lips. "You have yourself a deal."

She left, seeming entirely too pleased with herself. Probably plotting, if he knew her well, but he could handle her if she tried anything. He sat back, trying to focus. He was glad things had been squared away with Melinda. Maybe some closure there was a good thing.

He would fix things with Erin tonight when she came over.

So why did it feel as if the ground was crumbling beneath his feet?

CHAPTER SEVEN

ERIN

O N AUTOPILOT, ERIN threw her backpack into the passenger seat and pulled out of the packed parking lot. She spent the drive to her apartment going over the outline for her research paper. She'd been sketching it out for months. Now she could finally get feedback and start writing it. The thought excited her—and terrified her. It was only her entire future.

Maybe she could run her ideas by Blake tonight.

Tonight.

The company she started working for mostly did residential cleaning, but sometimes they asked her to clean a corporate office after hours. They had a standing date to see each other in the evenings she wasn't working. She had taken up the habit of showing up at his door with a DVD in hand. He'd order Chinese delivery, and they would eat greasy noodles and crack open a fortune cookie to share between them for good luck.

They'd only watch the first half of the movie because by the middle he would be kissing her and she'd have her hands down his pants. It had seemed like bliss only a few days ago. Now it all paled, darkened under the shadow of a woman from his past.

From the shadows of her own past that she'd never told Blake.

What did they really have in common? Great sex. That wasn't much to base a relationship on, especially when they needed to keep it a secret. Maybe Erin was blowing this out of proportion. Hopefully so. Old wounds causing pain in the winter. This could all mean nothing. Professor Jenkins meant nothing. Though still new and even fragile, her feelings for Blake felt breathtakingly real. That was all that mattered, wasn't it?

God, she hoped so.

She pulled onto the dappled concrete beneath the large elm tree. The apartments farther away from campus were much cheaper. Unlike the manicured gardens near campus, the beautiful foliage here was allowed to grow and bloom—even if it was only allowed to run wild to save on trimming costs.

Even the old building had a certain charm—

she imagined the mottled brown shingles and faded yellow shutters had been very pretty when they were brand new. And if she had to put up with the old pipes breaking every month and backing up questionable water onto her bathroom floor…well, she didn't really have a choice. This was all she could afford.

She unlocked the door and waved to Courtney.

Her friend and roommate didn't glance up from the thick, spread-eagle textbook. Her sleek, straight black hair fell around her face. "How was lover boy's first day?"

"Oh, swell."

Now Courtney did look up, her eyebrows arching in question. "Uh-oh, that doesn't sound good. What happened?"

If only Erin knew the answer to that. She grabbed an orange from the bowl and sat down. The sharp citrusy scent burst into the room as she pulled the peel away, invigorating her after the deflating ride home. "Well, things started off pretty good. Scratch that, *really* good."

"Sex?"

"Oh yeah. The best kind. Sort of frantic and breathless. And extra urgent because someone might have come in."

Courtney moaned. "Stop. I haven't been laid in like five years."

"You broke up with Derek a month ago."

"Yeah, but we hadn't had sex for a month before that."

Erin suppressed a smile. Two months wasn't very long in her book, considering she'd gone for two years without it before Blake. But she could understand better now. The orgasms, the intimacy—it was all so wonderful that she didn't want to go without it ever again.

"So," Courtney prompted, stealing one of the sections of orange and biting into it. "Great sex, and then?"

"And then Professor Jenkins stopped by." At her friend's blank look, she added, "She's one of the professors in my department. She's also on the board, which means she'll be one of the professors signing off on my final research paper. She has a reputation for being kind of mean, or at least harsh, but she always seemed nice enough. Or so I thought."

"The plot thickens."

"You have no idea. Because it turns out, she and Blake were...well, they were friends. Like serious friends. *Friends* friends."

Courtney cocked her head. "Why are you

saying it that way?"

"Some kind of relationship. It's not like they spelled it out for me with a line graph or anything. It was just there between them, thick in the air. Like they'd been lovers."

"How awkward."

"Then Professor Jenkins—Melinda, that's her first name—she starts going on about how they can go back to the way things were. While I'm still standing there."

"Even more awkward."

"Then Melinda asks me to leave."

Courtney gasped. "She didn't."

Erin waved her hand. "There was this weird excuse about me cleaning his office, because no one at the university is supposed to know about us, so she thought I was just working there. Anyways, I bolted before Blake could even explain anything, but I'm going over there tonight, and you have to tell me how to not freak out."

"Girl, you go ahead and freak out. I'm freaking out for you. I mean, you've been seeing him for like two weeks. Then the ex comes back in the picture? That's freak-out material."

"Surprisingly, this is not helping me calm down."

"You're trying to be rational and mature

about this? Sometimes I don't know why we're even friends."

"Trying is the operative word. I'm not succeeding very well."

Courtney looked sympathetic. "I know you were really into him. Are," she corrected herself. "You *are* really into him."

"Oh God," Erin moaned. "You think it's over? Should I not even go over tonight?"

"Of course you should go. Be mature and rational, yes. But also be sexy and irresistible, and *then* ask him what the deal is. I bet he's very happy with what he has now and was just taken by surprise when she was there. But if he turns you down, at least you'll leave him wanting more."

Erin looked down at her plain T-shirt and well-worn jeans. Her sneakers had turned grey and scuffed two years ago. "I don't really do sexy and irresistible."

Her friend smiled. "You do now."

ERIN

THE LACE-COVERED WIRE in the bra cut into Erin's sides, making it hard to breathe. The high-heeled shoes pinched her toes. It had taken a whole extra hour to get ready, but it was all worth it, because she had to admit, even to herself, that she looked pretty damn sexy. It wasn't an image she could keep up for any length of time, but then Blake was used to seeing her in drab, plain, well-worn workout clothes. The slinky black dress and heels were Courtney's. The lacy underwear was her own, something she'd grabbed in a bargain bin at the mall but forgot to wear for Blake before tonight.

She was dressed for battle, primed and ready to wage a sex war, where the only rules were pleasure and both of them would be victors. At least, she only hoped it led to a night of hot sex...not her walking out the door, leaving him "wanting more," as Courtney had said.

She turned off the main paved road onto the rough gravel one leading to his house. This wasn't exactly the country, still just twenty minutes from downtown Tanglewood. But somehow this area hadn't been populated thickly. Houses were sprawled across gently rolling hills, invisible at night, as if they were far from civilization.

Her old car grumbled softly as it bumped and jittered over the rough-hewn road. She patted the dusty leather dashboard. "You can make it, buddy."

She hoped so, anyway. She broke even every month, spending what she earned cleaning on her share of the expenses plus textbooks and food. There wasn't any margin for error, no room for a tired car to give out.

The farmhouse spread before her. It was relatively new and certainly large, but it was missing any pretension. Down to earth. Inviting and warm, like Blake.

The presence of another car parked off to the side squeezed her heart. A sleek blue roadster sat where Erin usually parked. It could have been anyone's car. But all her dread culminated, and she knew.

Professor Melinda Jenkins.

Please be wrong. Be somehow horribly mistaken about this whole thing. Maybe he has a friend over and didn't mention it when we talked about me coming over. Maybe Blake bought a new car sometime between his afternoon class and now.

Not likely.

She pulled her car up behind the other car and stepped out, grimly noting the contrast between the expensive car and her own. Surely that transmission had no problems running over gravelly roads. It probably purred while it went.

Her heels were shaky on the pebbled pathway.

That was something she hadn't anticipated. She decided to cross between the cars and use the sidewalk, something she didn't do often because it really wasn't all that convenient, shoved up against the house and overgrown, with palm leaves blocking the path.

But this way she could walk without tripping and falling on her face. The last thing she needed was to sprain her ankle and get caught out here. Stuck in another awkward three-way, watching Melinda make googly eyes at Blake while Erin did her best impression of invisibility.

Orange light glowed from the kitchen window. A particularly far-reaching agave plant nipped her ankle, and she stumbled, catching herself against the brick wall. As she turned her face up to the light, she froze.

Standing at the counter was Melinda, but not as she had been before. Not put together in a business suit with her hair pulled into a bun. This Melinda was wearing only a shirt, a white business type of shirt that hung to her thighs. Her red hair fell down her shoulders, clearly mussed. She looked like a woman who had just been made love to.

The same way Erin must have on the nights she slept over.

As if to twist the knife and plunge it deeper, Melinda picked up a white container of Chinese food and fished inside with a fork. She took a bite, tilting her head and chewing thoughtfully as if to gauge the flavors.

A cat-got-the-cream smile curved her thin, wide lips.

Erin's stomach churned, that familiar sick feeling of being on the outside looking in. God, she had wanted to believe it was all in her head. She had wanted to be wrong, but this was her nightmare, exactly so. Worse because of how comfortable Melinda looked...how smug. Erin didn't know what that would feel like to be so sure of her position, her desirability, her man's commitment to her that she could walk away and he'd be waiting when she came back.

Even in the fairy-tale hours after she'd first hooked up with Blake, she'd managed to push down the doubt—but God, it had been there. What if she wasn't pretty enough, smart enough? Rich enough? Not that Blake would ever be shallow, but the financial divide could manifest in many ways. She had learned that lesson the hard way.

Feeling a heavy weight and a sickening sense of history repeating itself, she carefully pushed away from the window and returned to her car. She pulled out slowly, half expecting Blake or even Melinda to come outside and see. Surely they would notice the headlights through the window or hear the car engine.

Maybe they were too wrapped up in each other to notice or care.

Disappointment was cold and slippery in her gut, a chilling companion for the ride back to her apartment. She parked in her usual spot, but instead of heading directly inside, she wandered over to the shaded courtyard. The night was cool for a walk, but she wanted that: the darkness, the quietude. She let it envelop her as she tripped along in her borrowed three-inch heels, gathering blisters on her feet for no reason.

The end of the courtyard was marked by nothing but a curb leading onto a sloping street. During the day this was busy, but now the road was empty. She could see lights glittering from downtown. Campus was indistinguishable from the rest of the city.

A bench had been installed beside a stop for the city's bus line. She sat down, feeling more contemplative than gloomy. The concrete reached through the thin fabric of her dress and chilled her.

What was she doing, getting all wrapped up in a man, in a relationship? Stress and drama. That wasn't why she was here. It wasn't why her mom cleaned houses twelve hours a day back in Laredo. Not why Erin herself busted her back at Blake's house and then for the company, taking extra hours cleaning the liberal arts computer lab when the custodial staff had vacation.

She was here to make something out of herself and her life, to be someone powerful enough that no one could mess with her—or her mother—ever again.

You and me against the world.

When she and Blake had first made love, it had been amazing, sensual, unlike anything she had experienced before. A high in contrast to the low she felt now, when she shouldn't be on the roller coaster at all.

So what now? Avoid him? She wasn't sure that was possible because his office was located in a building where she had some classes. Confronting him didn't seem like the right choice either. She didn't want to make him feel bad about any of this…but she'd have to do one or the other. She couldn't continue in limbo. He deserved a fair accounting from her.

With a sigh, she pushed herself up. Her skin

had goosebumped while she sat, and now she ran her numb fingers up and down her arms, trying to rub some warmth back into her. Her nipples had tightened in the cold, pressing through the thin material of her bra and dress. She crossed her arms and ducked her head against the wind as she slowly hobbled back.

Chapter Eight

Blake

B LAKE KNOCKED HIS head back on the brick
wall. The wind howled softly, starting to
pick up speed as the night wore on. The small
alcove in front of her door blocked most of its
bite, but he couldn't feel it over the coldness
inside.

Dread had built inside him, from the first
expression of shock on Erin's face, to watching
her flee down the hallway, him helpless to stop
her, through the long, agonizing day of watching
his new students whisper about what was wrong
with his face.

And he hadn't cared about the last part as
much as he'd thought he would because he was
too worried he'd screwed things up with Erin.

She was always cautious with him. Even when
they were making love, a part of her remained
guarded, waiting for him to lash out, and he
wanted to beat the shit out of whoever had made

her feel that way.

He tried to keep things as light as possible…which wasn't all that light where she was concerned, because he was crazy about her. So they made vague plans to meet up, and thankfully she'd pulled through every time.

Except tonight. He'd known something was seriously wrong when she'd left his office today. He had hoped to explain about Melinda…at least, as much as he could. Not the whole story, which would embarrass them both. Just enough so he and Erin could go back to the way things had been. But when she'd been later than usual, he'd known things weren't right.

He'd said *fuck it* to playing it cool and come to see her instead, except she wasn't here. He'd caught her roommate—he hadn't known she *had* a roommate—on her way out the door. At least he hadn't freaked the girl out too much. Courtney, she said her name was. She'd taken one look at his face and said, "Hi, Blake. Nice to meet you."

He raised his eyebrow. "My reputation precedes me."

"It does indeed." She winked. "But Erin's not here."

He ran a hand over his face, disappointed but ready to turn around when she stopped him.

"Wait here," she said, an almost playful expression on her face, hiding a smile.

He saw smiles rarely enough, and never from a stranger these days. "What?"

"Wait here for her to get back." She glanced back at the apartment. "I'm not sure I should leave you in here though."

"No, you're right to not let me in. We've never met before. I can wait outside."

She grinned. "Okay, stranger danger. But trust me. Erin wants to see you. And she should be back any minute, considering. I need to get to work anyway, so the apartment will be all yours." She had emphasized the last two words, as if she fully expected them to get busy in the small run-down apartment.

Well, he was on board with that plan, except that twenty minutes later there was still no sign of Erin. He remained in the doorway with an eye on his truck, determined to at least see Erin tonight. If she asked him to leave, well, then he'd go.

But he had to make sure she was okay. He felt her unhappiness like a physical weight around his neck. He didn't believe in that psychic aura stuff, but he'd had a sense of her feeling lost, alone, and he needed to try and fix that. Though maybe there wasn't any woo-woo explanation for it. Her expression when he'd seen her last was emblazoned in his mind: shock, hurt, betrayal. Things he remembered feeling when Melinda had left him.

He'd made Erin feel that way. Fuck.

"Blake?"

He jerked to the side, relieved to see Erin. He'd had a few words planned, but he was rendered speechless by the sexy black dress she was wearing. Electric lust shot through his body. He wanted to fall on her, to push her up against the wall and…

Fuck. He could restrain himself. He already looked like a monster.

He didn't have to act like one.

"Hey," he forced out.

"Uh…what are you doing here?"

Her eyes were guarded, and shit, had she been on a date with someone else? "I came to talk about what happened today."

If possible, she seemed to shrink in on herself even further. "Can't we talk about it tomorrow? I'm really tired."

His eyebrow rose. "On campus?"

That tugged a small smile from her. "Okay, I guess we should talk about it here."

He doubted he'd be able to keep his hands off

her inside her apartment, but he stayed silent as she unlocked the door and led him inside. The apartment was small and dark and threadbare. A standard college apartment, modest but comfortable, with thick plaid couches and plywood furnishings and a small potted plant blocking the television.

She caught his gaze. "We call him the Grumpy Geranium."

He tilted his head in question.

Wandering over, she touched a finger to the pink petals. "I'm not sure how it got started. I think we were drinking. I'm not huge on the party scene, but I'll go for wine coolers and a movie on Saturday night."

He hid a smile, imagining her tipsy. She was one of the most serious young women he'd ever met. He would like to see her more relaxed, more open. Of course, there was another way she became more lax, when they were in bed together…

He wasn't supposed to be thinking of that.

"Anyway, we named this plant the Grumpy Geranium because he looks kind of mad, don't you think?"

He looked doubtfully at the flowers. They looked…pretty?

She waved away the silent disagreement. "You had to be drunk. But basically he judges us until we've done all our homework and done the dishes and taken out the trash and *then* we can watch TV. He's like a guard." She rubbed a petal between her fingers before looking up, something strange and unsettling in her eyes. "You can sit down, you know. Sorry I didn't say so sooner."

Nodding, he found a seat on one end of the couch. She perched on the edge of an ottoman. A far cry from the close embrace they'd shared at his house.

Suddenly she looked ready to cry. His muscles tensed to go to her, but he wouldn't push her, not when she'd made the distance between them clear.

"I'm sorry about Melinda," he said soberly. "I had no idea she'd come by."

"But you knew she worked there." The statement was flat, not a question.

He took a deep breath. "As you may have guessed, we had a relationship. It's over."

"She didn't seem to think so."

He shook his head, still a little mystified. "I don't know why she thought I'd be open to that. Or why she would even want to start things up again. She's the one who broke things off. The truth is, it was more than dating. We were engaged."

"And she left you?" Erin sounded outraged on his behalf.

"Apparently getting married to the stuff of nightmares didn't appeal to her. That doesn't matter anymore. There's no chance of us getting back together. I made that clear to her when you left. I'm just sorry you had to be put in that awkward position."

"I can't believe she left you because of your scars."

"At the time they weren't really scars. They were burn wounds, not healed at all. Bright and even uglier than they are now, if you can imagine that."

Her eyes narrowed. "How soon after the explosion did she break up with you?"

"A couple weeks. I didn't blame her. She couldn't even bring herself to meet my eyes. Why would I want her to marry me after that? But it still hurt like a—well, it hurt a lot. They were dark times for me. I try not to think about it. That's why I never told you about her."

Curiosity lit her eyes. "Blake. Do you know where Melinda is right now?"

"No idea." He frowned. "She didn't talk to you about us, did she?"

"No," she said, and he felt relief. Then she added, "But I went to see you, and she was in your house, Blake. In your house, wearing your clothes and eating our takeout."

For a moment, he simply stared at her. Then he realized his mouth was hanging open. "Well, fuck. Why didn't you kick me in the balls when you first saw me?"

She shrugged. "I figured it wouldn't make a lot of sense for you to be here if you knew there was a half-naked woman back at your place."

Shit. He rubbed his brow. Erin had been coming to see him looking like some kind of sex goddess, and she'd found Melinda there. How had Melinda even gotten in? Though he hadn't changed the locks when she'd left him. He never expected her to come back.

"Erin, I had no idea she was there. I definitely didn't invite her."

"I believe you."

"I swear I didn't, Erin."

"I'm serious." She sighed. "I do trust you, despite my occasional ride on the insecurity train. It just took me by surprise, that's all. And then I got a little messed up inside. I never want to be that way, the jealous girlfriend asking where you went or who you were with."

"You have every right to be pissed, to doubt me—"

"No." She stopped him. "I never doubt you. I doubt myself."

He swallowed, steeling himself. "What'd the asshole do?"

She smiled, a little wry. "Am I that obvious?"

"I may not know everything that's happened to you, but I know someone hurt you."

Sadness darkened her eyes. It might not seem like a scarred professor had much in common with a beautiful college student, but their similarities weren't on the surface. They both knew about loss and about grief. About holding yourself together with the broken pieces. He wore the story of his pain on his skin, but hers was buried deep. He didn't know her secrets, but he was patient and determined. Eventually he would.

"It's incredible that you trust me, especially after what you saw. I don't think most people would have. I'm not even sure I could have so quickly. But there's something that scares you too, and I don't want you to have to hide that from me. You don't have to spare me anything. I want to see all of you, everything. I want to touch you, to kiss you—"

Her eyes brightened again. "Is everything

always about sex?"

"Around you? Yes. I deserve a goddamn medal for not touching you in that dress." She was liquid sex sheathed in desire, and he forced himself to recline on the sofa, stretching out his legs. Then he raised his eyebrows at her.

She put her elbows on her knees. "I shouldn't have gotten jealous."

"Yes, because the masses of women chasing me are truly a threat."

A fraying throw pillow was lobbed at him. With a small grin, he caught it and tucked it behind his head, still reclined on the sofa that was too small for him. He'd rather be holding her, but she needed the space. Besides, the damned furniture might buckle and break if she so much as breathed on him.

Looking far away, she said, "It was two years ago. Met a guy, started dating. The usual stuff. It seemed amazing. We got along great and we'd go to all these shows and museums...I couldn't afford to go out much, but he was pretty loaded and insisted on paying for me anyway. He said it was being a gentleman, no big deal. I was so eager to go with him I didn't really consider what the imbalance did to our relationship, the way he thought of me."

By slow degrees, Blake's muscles tensed with her retelling. He'd expected to hear the story of some idiot boyfriend who didn't appreciate her. Worst case, the asshole cheated on her. But he didn't like the sound of this at all. A rich guy pulling a subtle power play, charming at the beginning… That could go downhill fast, and he already knew this story had an unhappy ending.

"And the best part was—" The way she said it made it clear it meant exactly the opposite. "We came from the same hometown. Laredo. A small place but still big enough to have a few high schools, and I'd never met Doug before seeing him on campus. So that winter he drove us both back home in his Lexus, my stuff packed in the trunk alongside his. We were going to meet each other's families."

She paused, looking a little lost.

When the moment stretched, he prodded, "What happened, your parents didn't approve?"

Her laugh was hollow. "No, Mama didn't approve. But it was worse than that. We stopped off at his place first. His mom and dad were pretty nice to me at first. Naturally they asked about me living in town, where my mom lived, what she did. And found out she used to be their cleaning lady."

Hell. He hadn't even known her mother cleaned houses for a living. He could imagine that didn't go over well with the uptight assholes.

"Yeah," she said, correctly interpreting his grim expression. "His mom was kind of shocked, but his father was downright rude. He actually kicked me out. Asked me to leave."

Jesus. No wonder she'd been hurt by Melinda's words at the office today.

"Doug didn't defend me or anything. He drove me home and barely said a word."

Fuck it. She looked so small, so alone. He pulled her into his arms, pressing his lips to the crown of her head. "I never should have let her talk to you."

Erin took a shuddering breath, but she allowed him to hold her, even curled into him. "When I told my mom about it, she flipped out, saying I had to stay away from the whole family. We fought and finally she told me the reason why she stopped going there. Apparently when she had worked for them, Doug's father had hit on her…like really pushy. She said that's as far as it went, that she'd said no and then quit, but I don't think that's the whole story."

A shiver went down Blake's spine. Rape. That's what they were talking about, and Erin had been in this guy's house.

"I talked to Doug on the phone that night. His dad had some other messed-up story about my mom stealing something. We fought about it. Then he stopped taking my calls, even though he's the one who drove me there. The bus ride back took twelve hours."

"The fucker," Blake burst out, unable to hold it in any longer. When she jerked in his arms, he soothed her. "Sorry," he muttered.

She burrowed into his chest. "It's good to hear someone say that. I was half afraid you wouldn't believe me either. Honestly I was more shocked than anything. One day he's laughing and kissing me and making these promises about the future. And the next, it's like I'm dirt."

"He didn't bother you after that, did he?"

"Nope." She laughed, a little uneven. "I thought we were just having a fight. I mean, they were big problems, but I thought we were serious about each other. So we'd cool off over the winter break and patch things up later. Except when I got back to town, he avoided me. And then I saw him on campus with another girl. He didn't even look in my direction."

"Good riddance. Look, baby, I don't know whether this Doug is a predator or just a guy stuck with a shitty dad, but you know, you *know* it wasn't your fault or your mom's, right?"

"Yeah." She sighed. "I know, but it's hard to remember sometimes."

Realization sank in his gut. Cold self-disgust settled in his bones. "And then I came onto you like that guy did to your mother," he finished for her.

"No," she said, sounding surprised. "And then with you I can't seem to let my guard down even though I know you're nothing like him."

A grim smile twisted his lips. "Not totally different. I was still willing to use my position, my money to hold influence over you. I always knew it was wrong, but hearing about someone else doing it... Fuck. There's no question."

He was a bastard. He deserved for someone to kick his ass as surely as he wanted to beat the shit out of this Doug's dear old dad. And Doug, for being a pussy.

"Blake," she said, turning to face him. "I was grateful for the job, but it was my choice to show up for work each day. You didn't come on to me even when I wanted you to. You never pushed me to do anything at all."

Her sweet brown eyes met his directly, almost aggressively. She never flinched away from his scars, not in the beginning and certainly not now. Instead her expression was one of...tenderness. He hated to ruin it, but he couldn't lie to her anymore.

"Erin, I put an ad out for a housekeeper on a whim. I figured I might call someone in from time to time, but when I met you, I knew I had to see you again, so I set up a weekly cleaning schedule. Then that wasn't enough, so I increased it to twice a week. I'm as bad as Doug, doing whatever was necessary to keep you near me."

"Why?" she whispered, sounding genuinely confused. It broke his heart, that confusion, that despite the strength that attracted him to her, she didn't know her full worth.

"God, Erin. You're kind, you're smart. I knew it from the first day when you gave a mean, scary-looking guy a talking-to. You told me you would clean the house..."

"But you'd have to clean yourself," she finished.

"It had been a week since I'd showered," he admitted. "So I went upstairs and felt like a new man. And when I came back into the kitchen, you'd heated up soup for me to eat."

"All those pizza boxes were disgusting."

"I was disgusting," he agreed. Then softer,

"Though I think I've gotten better."

A smile played at her lips. "No more forts made out of pizza boxes."

"You noticed those, huh?"

"Yeah, you were a mess," she said with fondness. "But you do clean up nice."

He smiled too, then sobered. "I have no excuse for that, Erin. And I would understand completely if you want to break up with me…in fact objectively I think you should. But if you'd stay with me…God…"

"What?" she whispered.

He racked his brain for the right answer, the perfect gift that would bind her to him. And came up empty. "Nothing," he said roughly. "I have nothing to offer you. Only myself."

Her eyes filled with tears, and for a horrible second he thought she meant goodbye. Then she threw her arms around his neck and pressed her lips to his. After a second of shock and pure relief, he crushed her to him, kissing her as if his life depended on it, because as he felt her hair brush away the ever-present pain in his skin, he did depend on her. He knew only pain, and she was freedom. He felt madness, and with her it was pleasure.

He gathered her to him, reveling in the soft

weight and warmth of her in his arms again. She moaned and ground her sweet ass against his erection. He shoved the slinky fabric of her dress up her thigh, savoring smooth skin and the thin slip of her panties pointing downward. His fingers followed the edge, meeting the fleshy outer lips of her sex.

She gasped into his mouth. "*Blake.*"

"Yes," he grunted.

And he gave her more, at once lighter and harder, faster and deeper, until neither of them could take it anymore. He found her clit and pinched lightly. She exploded around him, a lovely feminine moan of ecstasy, a soft rush of hot liquid against his knuckles and the tremble of her thighs draped over his own.

He petted her softly as she came back down. His erection pulsed impatiently, straining against his jeans to get near her, but he forced himself to back up, to pull away before he impaled her. He had something to prove to himself if not to her. He could have a thoughtful conversation with her. He could watch a movie all the way through. Everything didn't always have to devolve into sex.

So when she turned those lust-dazed eyes on him and smiled sexily, he pulled the DVD case out of his jacket and held it up like a goddamned shield.

She blinked. "*Phantom of the Opera?*"

"You always brought a movie when you came over," he explained. "Since I was coming over, I wanted to bring something."

Her look was sweetly reproachful as she connected the characters. "Very subtle."

"Hey, it was either this or *Beauty and the Beast.*"

"At least in that one they end up together."

"Because he turns back into a normal man," he reminded her. "There are no happy endings for the beast."

Her expression dimmed. She crawled to him, straddling his legs with hers, and shit, how was he supposed to restrain himself like this? His dick was right there. A few layers of cloth could disappear and he'd slide inside her. She plucked the DVD from his fingers and tossed it to the side table.

"What are you doing?" he choked out.

She slid down to the floor between his feet. Her eyes flicked up, troubled and wicked. "Proving you wrong."

She proceeded to do just that, using her tongue and lips and breathy sighs to drive him to ecstasy. The truest form of pleasure, a pure and potent happiness that was not what he'd meant but so much better. He wanted this all the time; he wanted her forever.

Beneath her seductive touch, he trembled with need, with hope. But he'd wanted things before, and they'd exploded right in front of him. He'd dreamed these things before and woken up alone.

He tried to resist, to accept the satisfaction of having her in his arms without the promise of a future, but it overwhelmed him. Like a tidal wave it swept him along, dragged him under, further away until he couldn't see the shore.

There was only an endless expanse of him and her together, of sex and love and hope converging on the horizon. He was lost then, hips jerking upward in helpless thrall and coming copiously into her warm, waiting mouth. Dragging her onto his lap, he licked and suckled and teased her breasts until she rocked her hips down onto him. In barely minutes he was hard again, an aching erection ever ready to serve her need. It wasn't even about sex then but sharing. None of it mattered without her, not the beauty or relief.

He impaled her onto him; *this is what you do to me.* He pushed up into her; *feel me, take me, never let go.* Her mouth was open in wordless entreaty while her eyes…dear God, her eyes. They burned with something more poignant than lust—there was knowledge. She knew what she did to him with her body, how low he could fall. She knew how hopelessly he thrust into her, desperate for more of her all the while aware it would never be enough.

"Don't hide from me," she whispered.

But he didn't even know what she meant. He was looking at her. She could see the worst parts of him, in the ugliness of his face and the degenerate use of her body. He showed her every dirty, unkind desire and God help her, she never told him no.

He realized she was murmuring something. Not a wordless sex-chant, but something more. "Let me see, let me see," she moaned, and he shuddered beneath. He writhed, and it must have looked like pain. A tear slipped from the corner of his eye. A fucking tear—how had that happened? He didn't know, but it hovered there on the brink, and he was unable or unwilling to reach up and wipe it away. She wanted to see? He would show her what a coward he was, and even then he wouldn't let her go. *Mine.*

The teardrop slipped from his eye, falling over skin that should have died. But it wasn't dead, it was wholly, painfully alive. It burned all day and all night as if the explosion had never stopped. The moisture of a single tear wasn't nearly enough to put the fire out, but she rested her face against him, right there. Her soft skin was a balm anywhere, but there, on his burns, it was a goddamned miracle.

He'd stopped moving, he realized dimly, but she hadn't. She set her hands on his shoulders and moved over him in sweet, rhythmic sex. Her face was pressed against his, right where he was most disgusting, right where he was most vulnerable. He didn't know why she'd want to see that, but it twisted something inside him. It made him desperate.

Desperate, he grasped her shoulders and pulled her down. Too hard. She winced.

Shit. "Sorry," he muttered.

"No, that's what I... Show me."

He shook his head, refusing even while he held on tightly and did it again. She gasped at the impact, the breathy sound spurring him on. He thrust inside her faster and harder, the room filling with the slaps of her skin against his, of her moans and her cries. He was cruel and relentless but instead of turning him away, her sex clenched around him. It squeezed him tight as she threw back her head. Beautiful, so beautiful.

He shut his eyes tightly and placed hot, open-mouthed kisses at her neck while his body shuddered its release. He groaned against her skin, breathing her in while he ground her body down against his cock. Helplessly, his hand clenched in her hair. Her soft pussy tightened around his cock, her hips rocking gently, wringing a final spurt of come from his cock.

Her contented sigh was hot against his neck.

CHAPTER NINE

ERIN

CONSCIOUSNESS CAME BACK to Erin, carrying an almost acute sense of loss. The chill of something found and then lost. Still groggy, she stretched slightly, feeling along the thin cotton sheets of her bed. They were cool to the touch—and empty.

With a start, she opened her eyes, looking around for Blake. After their passionate bout of sex in the living room, they'd made their way into her bedroom for round two before falling asleep entangled in each other's arms. It was the first night he'd spent over at her place, the first time he'd been here at all, and though his house was certainly nicer, it felt lovely to have him here. Like the first burst of bright spring, blinding hope on well-worn terrain.

He wasn't in the bedroom or the bathroom. She slipped out of the bed, clothed only in the lingering musk from their lovemaking. A puddle of white turned out to be his undershirt. As she picked it up, something flat and square flipped open.

Little pieces of white floated down to the floor. His wallet. And she'd just spilled something. Bending, she started to gather the slips of paper when she realized what they were.

She opened one. *The key to your future lies in the past.*

Another. *All your hard work will soon pay off.*

Do not let ambitions destroy small successes.

Someone you care about seeks reconciliation.

There were more.

The fortune cookies. She swallowed past the lump in her throat. He'd saved the messages inside them, each and every one from their nights together. She was mildly impressed that some of them had come true, but far more moved that he'd kept these little folded pieces of paper, little notes of nothingness marking their time together.

Clutching the fortunes in her hand, she pulled the undershirt over her head. It went down to mid-thigh, so she padded out into the dark living room.

Blake stood at the sliding glass windows looking out, his silhouette both intimidating and forlorn. In that moment, she saw the warrior he usually kept carefully banked. His shoulders were broad and carved with muscles, angling down along thick arms crossed in front of him. His back was lean, sloping into loose-slung jeans he'd put on. His feet were bare, but she didn't discount his fierceness for one second like this. His deceptive casualness, his quiet intensity—he looked calm but ready to fight. Not murderous but capable of killing. She shivered.

The truth was that his time in the military wasn't a reality she understood. Throwing yourself into danger. Fighting for your life. It was theoretical to her. She felt in awe of his service to his country but unknowing of the harsh realities—or aftereffects.

Why didn't he sleep? She'd asked him that night in his study, but he'd never answered. She sensed the answer lay here, in the turmoil that rippled through the air unseen. He didn't sleep because he couldn't. He couldn't rest because his heart was still at war.

In some ways, it was a far greater barrier to their happiness than her mistrust of men, than Melinda, his lover-come-lately. The pain inside him was an invisible enemy that invaded when they were most vulnerable, breathing desperation into their intimacy and inevitably into their sex.

There were places inside him that she couldn't reach, not with her words or her body. And if she could? She was a little afraid of what she would find.

He turned suddenly, though unsurprised. She got the impression he'd known she was there, probably heard her wake up, his senses finely honed, primed for a battle left behind.

"Are you okay?" she asked softly.

"Why wouldn't I be?" he said, although it wasn't really an answer, she realized.

He crossed the room and took her into his arms. Some of the tension left his body, and she felt grateful at least that she helped him that much. If she could only be his balm, then she would soothe and soothe him until she was spread thin.

She opened her palm, showing him what she'd found. Some of the papers dropped from her hand, twirling in the still air like dandelion leaves, wishes on the wind.

"They fell out," she said. "You kept them."

He spoke gruffly. "I thought if I saved up, then maybe I could have a future with you."

Her yearning felt like a knife, slicing her into ribbons from the inside. A future, a together, a moment stretching out onto the horizon, never ending.

"Yes," she breathed, revealing her want.

"Yes?" he repeated, and she wasn't sure what he was asking for. A confirmation that they could have it, that they could last.

He'd told her he loved her on the first night they'd slept together. Never since, as if sensing how much she feared the undeniable pull of him, the sense that she could lose herself in him and never find her way out. With Doug it had been infatuation, but this was more—so much more. How much worse would it be to have him look at her with disgust? How much worse for him to pass her by on campus without even turning his head in her direction?

The memory of that winter break with Doug humiliated her, highlighting the worst parts of her life, how little she had to offer. She knew Blake didn't judge her for being poor, but the fact remained that she paid her rent by cleaning his large, stately home. Her mother scrimped and saved from her own cleaning business to help pay for the rest of her tuition not covered by the scholarship and loans. She was in a different stratosphere, miles away even as he held her close.

"Do you think love is enough?" she whispered, staring into his fathomless eyes.

For a moment he was silent, and she thought he might not answer. He seemed thoughtful and…so far away she'd never reach him.

He bent to press a kiss to her lips. "You pulled me back from the brink. I don't talk about it because I don't like to think about how close I was, how weak I was then, but it's true. And I never want you to feel beholden to me, stuck with me because I'd fall apart if you left. The fact is, losing you would hurt ten times worse than having half my face blown off, but I'd keep going. I'd go on living because I don't know any other way."

Her heart cracked a little then, an almost audible, tactile thing that filled her whole body with pain but also tenderness. A raw sort of hope, more jagged than love, more meaningful than all her fears.

"I love you, Blake."

"God, I know," he groaned against her forehead. "You can't know how much that means. Do I think love is enough? It's the only thing at all. The world is cold and hollow, but with you, I feel alive again."

A tear slipped down her cheek, meeting his bare skin, dampening the crinkly hair and muscled plane of his chest.

"Ah, don't cry, Erin. I never meant to make you cry."

"I can't help it. I just want so much…I need…"

"Shh," he soothed her, walking her back into the bedroom, pressing her down on the bed. They were numbing the pain, they were pushing the worry out of focus to be dealt with another day, but she didn't care.

There was only so much she could take, that he could take before he needed release. Before she needed to give it to him.

He murmured to her, *don't cry, never cry, love you, love you*, and she found that she wasn't the balm after all; it was him. She wasn't the one to heal him; she was put back together with each soft touch and firm invasion of his body into hers. *Let go*, he whispered, and she wasn't held together anymore; she broke apart. She fell to pieces, awash in a sea of sweet senses, a land with no edges and no divides—just this.

Just bliss.

CHAPTER TEN

ERIN

ERIN PICKED UP her clothes by the dawn's pale light and left Blake's room, shutting the door behind her. She slipped into the bathroom down the hall to change. She didn't want to wake Blake. No, that was a lie. She wanted very much to wake him up, to make love to him, and to spend the rest of the day in bed with him. But real life was on her heels, right upon her.

Two weeks of bliss tore down her every defense.

Real life was here to build the walls back up again.

Final professor assignments were announced today, and that meant textbooks would be listed in the university's bookstore bulletin. She needed only one class for her last semester. The rest of her credits were for research, though in truth, the exploratory phase was complete. Now she had to write the final draft of her thesis, which would be presented to the committee at the end of the summer semester.

She splashed water on her face and looked at herself in the mirror. College graduate. Barely making ends meet. Master's degree candidate. Maid service. She didn't know which side was the real Erin.

She left the bathroom and paused outside the closed door. All was quiet. She continued on without disturbing him. It was so early. *Let him sleep.*

The stairs were dark. She trailed her fingertips on the wall to find her way. Downstairs, she grabbed a banana from the bowl in the kitchen to eat on the drive home. In the shadowed foyer, she bent to slip on her shoes.

"Leaving without a goodbye?"

She turned at the low sound of Blake's voice. He must have followed her downstairs, stealthy like a soldier. "You scared me."

"I'm sorry," he murmured.

She took a step toward him, hesitant. "No, I'm sorry for waking you."

They were both lying. He didn't like it when she slipped away, and she didn't either. He came forward as she leaned closer. Strong arms pulled her to him. She rested her cheek against his bare chest, her sigh of relief mingling with his.

It was always a strain to leave him, even knowing they would see each other again soon. Perhaps because their relationship had to be secret. Their passion, their love for each other, existed only in the circle of their embrace.

She breathed him in, his sleepy male scent and faint musk of sex. Her body still hummed with remembrance of his touch, his tongue. His cock. Which was currently pressing against her hip.

She hid her smile against his neck. Morning wood was like God's gift to women. Softened by sleep everywhere, except for there, hard and ready. What a beautiful way to start the day. Even at 6 a.m., he was primed for her, holding her tighter as her sex grew warmer, their bodies communicating in an ancient language. Her pulse, his groan. She pressed her lips to his collarbone. He crowded her back against the wall.

"I've got to go," she said, even while she let her purse drop to the floor. Her wallet fell open on the tile, pens scattered as the contents spilled out, but she didn't care about anything as long as he held her this way, as long as he surrounded her and ached with her. As long as they were together.

"Stay with me. Never leave." He turned his words into action, pushing his hands beneath her shirt and tugging it over her head. He groaned at the sight of her bare breasts.

She bit her lip. "I couldn't find my bra in the dark."

He cupped one breast reverently. "Beautiful."

She squirmed against the wall, aching for more. He was too gentle, too soft. He did it on purpose, the bastard. His tender admiration drove her crazy. She wanted *more* and *harder* and *faster*, and all he gave her was reverence.

But she was not without power here. His body awoke whenever she was near, heating up, growing taut. The muscles of his chest rippled beneath her touch. His jaw clenched when her thumb gently scraped his flat nipple.

He unzipped her jeans, and she slid them off with a wriggle of her hips.

"I really do have to go," she said, more breathless this time and with far less conviction.

"I know. Just saying goodbye."

"Is that what they're calling it these days?" Her laugh was cut short when he slid two fingers between her legs, testing her—and finding her, she knew, slick and ready.

Her sex still felt swollen and tender, not yet recovered from the pounding he had given her last night. Nothing like now. This was slow and lazy, but somehow just as urgent. Somehow more poignant, as he hitched one of her legs on his hip.

Only a little foreplay this time. His fingers testing her, probing her. Then he pointed his cock to her core. She wound her other leg around him, and he slipped inside. She was supported by her arms around his neck, by his broad hands beneath her ass, by the wall at her back. Held suspended on his cock, writhing and wishing and begging for him to move.

God, she needed him to thrust inside her, but she was completely at his mercy. And sometimes he could be a real bastard. A horrible tease. He nibbled his way down her neck, as if they were going to make out now instead of fuck. She wanted him so badly that she tensed up—she clenched around his cock. He growled and pushed inside her, deep and fast. She gasped from the shock and pinch of pain.

"Sorry," he murmured, and unlike earlier, she heard true regret in his voice.

"More. Like that."

"I'll hurt you."

Yes, she wanted that too. "Fuck me, Blake."

He shuddered in her arms. He always loved when she spoke dirty to him.

She rocked her hips, the only movement she

could make. "Fuck me like you can't take it anymore."

His dark eyes burned. Slowly, achingly, he pulled back—and plunged in to the hilt. They both moaned at the complete and intimate contact. Stuffed full of his cock, impaled on his body, and yet yearning for more. Never enough.

She whispered in his ear. "Fuck me like you're mad at me."

With a pained groan, he let go. He shoved her hard against the wall and rammed inside her. Her body was held still, pinned by his, her mouth open on a silent cry of painful pleasure. His cock moved inside her, invading her, hurting her—and God, she never wanted it to stop. Never wanted to feel *empty* and *nothing* and *unwanted* again. This was desire and craving. It was consuming.

Tendrils of ecstasy threaded through the roughness, teasing her orgasm, drawing it out until she sobbed with needing it, until she called his name. *Blake, fuck me, fuck me. Fuck me, Blake.* It was a chant, a prayer, but he was too far gone to hear her, too far above her to answer.

He froze on a choked cry, pouring his seed into her. The twitch of his cock within the swollen tissue of her sex pushed her over. She let go in a rush of liquid and stuttered moan, tightening around him and wrenching a startled gasp from him. They held each other in the aftermath, their sensitive flesh pulsing against the other, his breath hot on her shoulder.

"Jesus, Erin." He leaned on her a little, still rocking in a lazy rhythm. "You killed me with that. You fucked the life right out of me."

Her laugh came out husky. "That's because you're not supposed to be awake yet."

"So come back to bed."

"I have to go to the bookstore. They're going to have the textbooks listed today, and the professor assignments. Maybe I'll see your name up there."

"Don't remind me." He gently lowered her to the floor.

"This will be awesome, I promise. There's still time for you to practice your lecture for me."

"You get bored when I lose my shit about Tiberius Gracchus."

He did get worked up over it. Tiberius Gracchus sounded like a smart and progressive leader, at least the way Blake told it, and it was pretty depressing that he'd been violently murdered for it. But Blake's anger didn't seem diluted by the fact that this had happened in the 2nd century BC.

"I don't mind when you talk about it." She

blushed, remembering when he'd translated some dirty insults from Latin. "Especially if you read me more from *Martial's Epigrams*."

He snorted. "I must admit, U.S. history lacks a certain passion compared to Rome's."

"Come on, let me hear your lecture."

"No way. I can make a fool of myself in front of a bunch of strangers. I don't have to do it in front of my girlfriend."

She couldn't help it. She grinned, sudden and wide.

He cocked his head. "What is it? Morning breath? You should have told me."

She rolled her eyes. "No, you called me your girlfriend."

"What else should I call you?"

"Hmm. Your fuck buddy?"

He frowned. "My lover."

"Your maid." No matter that she didn't work for him anymore. That was how they met. It would always define their relationship, wouldn't it? It would always be between them.

His hands clasped hers. He rested his forehead against hers. "My everything."

She sighed in happiness. Maybe everything would be okay.

BLAKE

BLAKE LEANED AGAINST the doorframe and watched until her red taillights turned onto the main road. It was best that she leave. He had a lot to take care of, and it would be too tempting to lose himself in her body while she was near. She'd helped drag him out of the pit he'd dug for himself, and he was grateful. But he couldn't continue to use her as a crutch. Already he felt the stirrings of hope within him, like a breath of spring wind. He'd catch himself thinking of someplace to take her, fitting in travel plans between his terms at the university. Terms, plural. As if he'd stay on, when he swore it was only temporary.

All of that was well and good, but before he could move forward, he needed to look back. To finally handle what he'd been too fucked up to deal with when he'd first returned home.

The drive to the hospital took thirty minutes, during which time he steeled himself. Still, as the wide automatic doors slid open, the chemical smell hit like a physical blow. He gritted his teeth and stepped inside. The muted conversation between the nurses, the fluorescent lighting, the mauve-beige-neutral walls—all too fucking familiar. He broke into a cold sweat, feeling the searing pain of his burns all over again. Months, he'd lain in that bed. He remembered shouting hoarsely for them not to touch him, to just give him more pain medicine and go the fuck away. They hadn't listened, poking and prodding.

"Sir?"

He blinked. A nurse in pink scrubs was staring at him.

"Are you okay, sir?"

"Yes. Yes, of course. I'm looking for a friend of mine."

She led him to the information desk where she looked up Private First Class Joseph Davis. Blake had visited when he'd first been discharged, but as he'd suspected, Joe had been moved to a different room. A different wing altogether, a more permanent one.

Pink and blue balloons in the gift shop window caught his eye. He stopped inside and picked out a small arrangement of colorful flowers. Joe wouldn't care—or notice—but he suspected Sherry would be there.

The room was much nicer than the old one had been. It was large, with faux cherry-wood paneling, a wide window overlooking the city, and a sofa that probably doubled as a bed. He studiously avoided the bleached white hospital bed in the center of everything, crowded with plastic piping and holding the unconscious body of his friend.

Sherry stood and greeted him with a tired smile and no surprise to mark the months that had passed. "Blake, how are you? Come in, come in."

He handed the flowers to Sherry and gave her a kiss on the cheek. "You look great. How's the kiddo?"

"Don't think I didn't notice you deflecting. But thanks. Matt's at school."

"School? Jesus. Last time I saw him he was in diapers."

She laughed, setting the flowers down by the window. "Preschool. They do colors and shapes and stuff, that's all. Just twice a week. Gives me some time to breathe."

"Of course you need a break. In fact, you should let me hire someone. I can't believe I didn't think of that before."

"Blake, you've already done too much for us."

"I haven't been here in months."

She rolled her eyes. "And who paid off the mortgage on our condo?"

"I got your thank-you note. That was sweet." She'd signed her name at the bottom…and his.

Joseph and Sherry Davis. Blake had gotten drunk and surfaced a week later with a mother of a hangover.

"Well, come on. You can talk to him. I'll run and grab some coffee. You want something?"

"I'm good. Take your time."

She flashed him a smile as she grabbed her purse. The door closed behind her.

Finally Blake allowed his gaze to find the center of the room. An accordion base and plastic rails. Thin white sheets. A drip from a clear bag to his vein, keeping him alive. Joe hadn't wanted that. Blake had suggested that to Sherry when he'd visited her then. He thought she would have slapped him then if he hadn't been wrapped three times around with bandages. So here they were.

He strolled to the side of the bed and sat down. Sherry would give him enough time. She may not always agree with what they wanted, but she understood them. Soldiers. Survivors. She was both as well.

"Hey, man." His voice cracked. He cleared his throat. "It's me. Blake."

His chest felt tight. This was harder than he thought. Which was saying something, because he'd thought it would be pretty fucking hard.

The machinery beeped in the background.

Unobtrusive, he supposed. He wondered if Joe could really hear anything. He wondered if the beeping was driving him insane.

Joe's face was slimmer and clean-shaven. It bore none of the bruises and marks that Blake remembered. No scars. Unlike Blake, his wounds were all inside. Irony had painted their lives with broad, cruel strokes.

Blake wasn't much older, but he'd already gone through a couple tours. He was the corporal, team leader, and occasional mentor to the new kid. Joe had looked up to him like he was Indiana Jones, and without fully realizing it, Blake had eaten that shit up.

Then they'd gotten blown apart. Well, Blake's face had gotten blown up mostly. He'd woken in a dank, dark prison, finding both himself and Joe tied down like animals.

Only then, the craziest fucking thing happened. Blake was the team leader. He knew way more valuable shit. He should have taken the brunt of the interrogation. *He* should have been the one tortured. Except he was out of his mind with pain from the burns, delirious and incoherent. So they'd focused all their attention on Joe. Young, guileless Joe.

They were rescued in two weeks. Just a blip

on the radar. Two weeks, fourteen days, 336 hours of torture. On the official forms, it said there were two survivors. But only Blake had woken up, his face so ruined that his fiancée had walked out at the first sight of him. Meanwhile, Sherry had stayed by Joe's side all this time. She'd never give up, and Joe would never wake up, so yeah. Irony was a bitch.

Beep. Beep. Beep.

He swallowed. "I met someone. Her name's Erin. It's pretty serious. She makes me…well, she makes me want to be better. That probably sounds strange, because I know I told you all about Melinda back then."

Deep breath. It got easier, he was finding, if he kept going. Maybe there was a lesson in that. Just keep moving forward.

"It didn't work out. She left me, really. But she was right about one thing. We couldn't have gone back to the way things were." He hadn't fully understood that at first. Not even when she hadn't come to pick him up from the hospital after he was released. Instead she'd been waiting at the door to his house. He'd been so overwhelmed and lonely after months in the damn hospital bed. He'd pulled her into his arms. She hadn't hugged him back.

Then he'd noticed the luggage.

"I know I'm an ass for even talking to you about this. I get to walk around and live my life. A different one. I wish I could give that to you, man. I wished for so long that I could trade places with you." But he couldn't, and so for a while he'd stopped living his own life.

Beep. Beep. Beep.

"Sherry looks great, by the way. Really..." Steadfast. Loyal. Kind. And it was fucking weird feeling any amount of envy for a man in a coma. "Really lovely. Just like you said."

Through the window, he could see gray clouds weighing down over the city. It would rain later.

"I'm sorry it took me so long to come back. I was being a dumbass, but you've probably figured that out by now. I'm going to try and be better. Check in on Sherry and the kiddo more often. Everything's okay out here, so you...you don't have to worry. Just focus on getting better."

He reached out and squeezed Joe's hand before he left. Sherry stood outside the room, chatting with the nurses. He hugged her goodbye and promised to visit in a week.

It had been a type of lie, what he'd said to Joe. *Just focus on getting better.* The odds were he would never get better. The doctors had said as much. Sherry had refused to believe that. And maybe Blake didn't quite believe it either. As he walked into the overcast day, he felt a little bit lighter.

CHAPTER ELEVEN

ERIN

ERIN HAD ALWAYS known she'd go to graduate school, even in high school, even though no one in her family had gone to college at all. She wanted to work in the political sphere, behind the scenes. And though she was prepared to do grunt work at the bottom, she aimed higher. Her master's degree would be a statement of intent, telling the world—and herself—that she was damn serious.

She returned to her apartment in the prime hours of morning. The tiny kitchen was silent and cheery, sun streaming through the windows. It was starting to look foreign to her. She'd spent the past few nights at Blake's house.

A hot shower washed away any trace of Blake's lovemaking from her body. She moved quietly so as not to wake her roommate, granting Courtney a few extra minutes of sleep. Soon enough she could wait no longer.

She rapped on the door lightly, just in case Courtney had already gotten up. When she heard nothing, she went inside.

Her friend was tangled up in the sheets, snoring softly.

"Wake up, sleepyhead. Time to get our books." A few more tries were required before a pillow was launched at her. She caught it and tossed it back to the foot of the bed. "Come on. Up and at 'em."

Courtney squinted at her. "You're evil."

"Hey, if you want to drive to campus by yourself…"

"No, I'm up."

"Okay, because you're still not moving."

"Any second now, I swear."

"I'm sorry, sweetie. I wouldn't do this to you, but you know they'll run out if we don't get there early."

That wasn't strictly true. The university bookstore never ran out of the required textbooks—just the used copies, which were all Erin could afford.

One semester Erin hadn't had enough to cover the five-hundred-dollar total. Courtney had offered to charge one of the books to her card, saying her parents would never notice. But even if she paid the money back, it felt too much like charity. So Erin had visited the library every few days to use the in-house copy for her assignments.

Courtney dragged herself out of bed and stumbled into the bathroom. Erin returned to the kitchen and looked over the notes for her research paper while she waited. In ten minutes, her friend emerged with damp hair, sweatpants, and a tank top that said *DON'T HATE* in glittery letters.

Dark sunglasses shielded her eyes, though she was still indoors. She looked like a rock star going out to fight the paparazzi.

Erin stifled a laugh. "That bad, huh?"

Courtney stuck out her tongue. She shuddered as they entered the sun and made their way to Erin's car. "I didn't get home until three. And this is why Jägermeister is a bad idea, boys and girls."

"I think I've heard this PSA before," Erin said, pulling out of the parking lot.

"Yes, well, I can't seem to learn my lesson. Plus Derek was there, so things got a little crazy."

Derek was Courtney's ex...and of course he was there. Some said it wasn't a party until he arrived, so Erin wondered why she kept going to them. Except she knew exactly why. They were on-again-off-again, and Courtney would prefer them to be on. Again.

"You know you should leave him alone."

She gave Erin a glare that said her hangover was still going strong. "You're one to talk. Dating the professor."

"He's not *my* professor."

"Ohh," Courtney said in mock-relief. "In that case, everything is hunky-dory. So I guess you told your mom about him."

Erin slanted her a look, and Courtney laughed. No, she hadn't told her mom. It would only make her worry.

"I'll tell her soon. She can meet him when she comes for graduation." Her mother might be annoyed when she figured out how long they'd been dating, but she'd come around, especially once she met Blake.

"Hey, I'm just giving you a hard time. I think it's a good thing. Everyone needs to do something a little wild while they're in college. Or in my case, many things."

"But you always tell me what a bad idea it was."

"Sure, *after* the fact. It's usually fun while it's happening. Do as I do, not as I say."

"Hmm." Though she wouldn't have imagined it just a year ago, she was indeed following in

Courtney's fun-loving, impulse-indulging footsteps. Surpassing them really, because even Courtney hadn't banged a professor.

It didn't bother her on its own. She'd never been a stickler for propriety, and the way she felt about Blake far outweighed any lingering concerns over bylaws. But keeping it a secret crossed some line she hadn't realized she'd drawn. The old Erin had put her mother and college career first. This new Erin...she didn't know her too well. The one who got fucked against a wall at dawn. Who was she? It was fun and exciting, but everything had to balance out in the universe. A childhood of secondhand clothes and sewn-up backpacks taught her that nothing came for free. So what was she trading in for this newfound bliss?

The parking lot was already packed full of expensive, shiny cars and yawning students making their way to the university bookstore's entrance. Inside, she and Courtney split up amid the metal bookshelves and large crates of text-books.

They'd clearly arrived with time to spare. The place looked well stocked, and besides, Erin only had the one book to find. Her other credits were for her research. No textbook required for that, just many, many regular books at the library which she'd practically memorized by now.

She felt guilty for rushing Courtney out the door. It had been habit and an early-onset case of nostalgia that had her rushing over here. Four years of undergrad and two in graduate school. She would miss this place.

She trailed her finger along the cool metal shelving, feeling the harsh edge where one stopped and the next began. The school was beautifully appointed, with gorgeous oak desks and hardwood flooring. But the basement of the bookstore, where the textbooks were kept, was little more than a warehouse. Strangely, she felt most comfortable down here, strolling through towers of books.

She found the right aisle and made her way down. Ah, here it was. *Quantitative and Analytical Political Science*. Her last official class, not counting her research. She scanned the small printed paper. Her heart stuttered.

Dr. Blake Morris.

She read it again. That couldn't be right. But oh God, oh God, of course it was him. The professor's name had been left blank when she registered for the course. It wasn't unusual. The tenured professors had their preferred courses to teach, but the adjunct staff was juggled around each semester. This was the course they'd hired him to teach. Her class. His specialty was U.S. history! She'd just assumed… Hadn't he mentioned the Romans…? He was always talking about the Romans. She thought that would be classical history. Maybe even archeology.

Philosophy? Oh God. She was so screwed.

Her earlier words to Courtney came back to her in a sick rush. *He's not* my *professor.* She felt like she was going to throw up all over the shiny textbooks.

In a trance, she paid for the book and stumbled outside to the curb. She stared at the loose gravel on the street, the weeds poking up between the slabs of concrete.

Courtney found her. "Hey, I looked everywhere inside."

"Sorry."

Her friend sat beside her. "What's wrong, sweetie? You're pale as…well, as I probably am right now. But that's because my blood alcohol level is still through the roof, most likely."

Erin forced a small smile. "It's his class. The one he's teaching. The one I'm taking."

She was babbling, but Courtney got the picture. "Shit, are you serious? What are you going to do?"

Well, that was the question. Blake had signed a contract to teach this course. His reputation and professional future depended on him following through. Maybe also his sanity, considering how he'd been cooped up for so long. Not to mention all the students who would be stuck if he backed out.

And she...she needed this class to graduate. Could she put it off, wait another semester?

She hated that she was even considering delaying her graduation. Objectively she knew Blake's situation was far more weighty and precarious. Her life would be little changed whether she graduated at the end of this summer or after the fall semester instead. But just thinking about it made her burn. She had worked too hard for this. Her mother had worked too damned hard to give her this opportunity.

Besides, she wanted desperately to be on equal footing with Blake. That could only happen once she graduated.

"Nothing," she finally said. "I'm not going to do anything."

Courtney stared at her. "But he'll be your professor. Like, in the same classroom."

"I know."

"He'll be *grading* you, Erin."

"I know. He'll do it fairly. He wouldn't be able to do it any other way."

Courtney looked dubious. "I think you're underestimating the persuasive power of our girl parts, but let's put that aside for a minute. You don't think that would be a little…I don't know, uncomfortable? He'll be your teacher. Don't hate me, but it's kind of a turn-off."

Erin almost laughed. His position was a massive turn-on for her. They'd role-played the parts a few times before. Always playful and teasing, never with any real force behind the scripted words. Even now, she imagined he would look incredibly hot standing up there, lecturing. That was one of the reasons she'd wanted him to practice on her. Except he hadn't wanted her to see. That was the worst part. He didn't want her to see that side of him, the real side, for one afternoon, and now she would sit in his classroom every day for six weeks. At least it was only that and not a full semester. She wasn't sure either of them could survive three months of it.

"Look, I pushed him to do this. He didn't want to. He did it for me. So now if he backs out and has to deal with the professional backlash, that'll be my fault. I'll feel horrible about that, and even if he doesn't at first, he could wind up resenting me. Hell, he *should* resent me."

"I'm resenting you a little," Courtney offered.

"Thanks," Erin said drily.

"Okay, but what if he just explains that there's a conflict of interest? Surely they won't hold it against him if he has a good reason."

"They'd probably hold him to his contract and drop me from the class. Besides, I can't embarrass him that way. Everyone would find out. We've got to keep it a secret until I graduate. Then they can say whatever they want. So that's why I *need* to take this class. Sooner rather than later."

"Oh, sweetheart. I don't want this to be something you regret. It's good to be wild and have great sex and all that jazz. Believe me, I know. If it were me, I'd do this in a heartbeat. I'd make dirty jokes all through class. I'd pass him notes and wear my shortest skirts in the front row. But that's not you."

No, that wasn't Erin. She'd had sex in Blake's university office, just once, and it wasn't likely to ever happen again. She liked being wild and having great sex and all that jazz, as Courtney had put it, but she preferred it in the privacy of Blake's home. In that way, they were well matched. He lived like a recluse, and she wanted to seclude herself with him. But the world would intrude and demand its due. And it demanded that he teach this class and she take it. Not a big ask, really. She'd dealt with worse. Hey, it could even be fun. And educational. She'd bet he was a great professor. So thoughtful and enthusiastic—and stern when it was warranted.

Oh God, the thought of him reprimanding her made her hot.

BLAKE

SHE WAS HIDING something. Blake knew it, but he didn't feel compelled to push her. He'd made dinner. Spaghetti wasn't a gourmet meal, but it was a step up from takeout or pizza. He'd even dug in the back of his pantry for a bottle of wine. They were enjoying a quiet evening. She would tell him what she needed to when the time was right.

Now more than ever, he knew how much he wanted to keep her. Knew it with a bone-deep certainty. Since his visit to Joe, some of the urgency had faded. That drive to possess her, hold her like she might slip away if she weren't clenched tightly enough. Here in the sweet current of her company, he saw things with more clarity—with a little more faith in the future.

She took a sip. "This is good. Is it a special wine?"

He raised his eyebrows. "Special how?"

"I don't know. You seem like the kind of guy who'd know about wines. Labels and wine tastings and stuff."

He shrugged. "It's Merlot. My mother is the wine enthusiast, and I mean that in the best and worst way. But that has nothing to do with who I am. I'll serve Kool-Aid next time if you want it."

She grinned. "You drink Kool-Aid?"

"What, everyone likes Kool-Aid. It's a child-hood staple."

"Oh my God, you must have been an *adorable* kid. I can see it. Little Blake wearing his leading strings and suspenders."

He snorted. "Exactly how old do you think I am?"

"I don't know…but old." She blinked innocently. "Like thirty?"

He threw the crust of his breadstick at her.

She ducked, laughing. "Thirty-one?"

Hiding his grin beneath a scowl, he rounded the table. "I may be ancient, but I'm still strong enough to deal with a mouthy little girl."

"Feeling spry, are you?"

"That's it." He lifted her bodily from the chair and carried her into the living room. He didn't let up even when he tossed her onto the couch. He followed her down and—he felt this was the only logical rebuttal of her accusations—tickled her until she was breathless and panting in his arms. Exactly as he liked her, laughing and so fucking perfect it made his heart hurt.

He pulled back slightly, feeling oddly reticent, like he couldn't let himself reach too far. Which was crazy, because this was Erin. His Erin, his girl.

Her smile faded. She put a hand to his cheek, stroking gently. "What's wrong?" she asked.

"Nothing. Sorry."

"Don't keep it from me, whatever it is. Remember? Every part of you and every part of me."

She looked up at him in the dim light spilling over from the dining room. Her dark golden hair framed her face against the brown leather of the couch. He wished her eyes weren't so wide, her lips weren't so full. He wished he could turn away.

Instead he stared back, his mind racing with words like *steadfast* and *loyal* and *kind*. With *lovely*. He understood it now. So much more than how she looked or talked, though that was part of it. *Every part of her*, and he wanted to drown himself in every sweet, doleful inch.

"You're so beautiful," he said thickly, because it was all he could say.

Something flickered in her eyes. Wariness. Guilt? What was she keeping from him?

But she kissed him, pressed those lush lips to his, and he let her. Let her slip the invisible blindfold over his eyes and let her, let her, because he trusted her. Even if it made him an idiot, he needed to trust in that dark place where he'd been beaten and burned and come out stronger this time.

She tasted faintly of wine, rich and velvety. He recognized notes of chocolate and red fruit, because he was exactly as stuffy as she'd thought he was. He'd only had Kool-Aid on the occasions he'd gone to friends' houses, but that was all in the past. From before. He hadn't died in that godforsaken bunker, but he'd been reborn. He was a different man now, a better one.

He slipped his hand behind her neck, reveling in the silky strands between his fingers, in the delicate nape cradled in his palm. He felt suffused with her softness, bruised and beaten by it. How could she accept him so fully? But she did. She pressed her cheek against him, right where he was most mangled. Her skin was cool, soothing him. Marking him, like he wanted to do for her.

He stood up, leaving her sprawled and languid on the sofa. The purple dress she wore hugged her curves and rode up her thighs—it had to go. He pulled it off her, careful not to tug her hair and not letting her up either. Her bra and panties went next so that she lay on the soft, cool leather wearing only her black heels.

If he could paint her like this, he would. Make her stay in this position for hours while he stood behind the shield of an easel, capturing a part of her for himself. Instead he could only look at her, burning the memory into his brain. But hell, already he'd never forget. He knew every color of her skin, from the pink of her nipples to the pale porcelain of her belly. The tanned slope of her shoulder and the golden hairs behind her neck. He had catalogued her like the most diligent of researchers, leaving little notes scribbled in the margins. *Here she's sensitive but she likes to be licked. And there, God, she can come right there.*

A brief squeeze of her wrist told her to stay. He retrieved a glass of wine from the dining table. *Is it a special wine?* she'd asked, and yes it was. He would never again be able to taste it without tasting her too.

He dipped his forefinger in the drink and touched her nipple, allowing the deep red liquid to coat her puckered skin. He'd meant to paint her all over first, but impatient lust had him mouthing her breast, swirling his tongue around the tip, and sucking on her. The other one was delicious as well, the dry, spiced wine contrasting with the sweet, fresh flavor of her.

Her eyes were hazy with arousal. Her legs had fallen open in sumptuous abandon. *Take me*, they said, and fuck yes, he was going to. He tipped the glass and poured a small puddle onto her belly. Muscles quivered beneath his lips as he lapped it up, dipping his tongue into her belly button.

Her legs were spread wide now, one of her feet on the floor, the other inching up the back of the couch. She was asking him to touch her, begging him with her body. He set the wineglass on the coffee table.

She groaned. "Please, Blake."

Jesus. He loved the sound of her, everything she said, everything she didn't say.

"Shh," he soothed.

He loved to make her come, but she was burning up now. On the edge. He could bring her higher, but only with patience. He tucked a throw pillow under her head before shedding his clothes.

She watched from beneath gilt-tipped lashes, a small, appreciative smile on her face.

Leaning over the couch, he aimed his cock at her mouth. She opened for him obediently, her dark gaze flicking up to him. The wet heat, the searing lust in her eyes, was like a vise to his balls, wrapping them up so tight he almost came right then. He shut his eyes and forced it back. *Not yet.*

Her tongue swirled around the head of his cock. Her mouth had always been amazing, but it was more poignant now that she had knowledge of his body. He hadn't been the only one taking notes. She slid her tongue along the slit, and stars bloomed behind his eyelids. She scraped the underside with the flat of her tongue, and he groaned, long and low.

"Fuck, baby. Fuck."

She sucked him eagerly, pulling him in, and his hips moved forward of their own accord. He found his way inside with small, nudging thrusts, tunneling his way into the incredible warmth. It wasn't enough. She was still tugging on him, her suction a small, feminine plea.

He raised an eyebrow. "You want more?"

With her lips wrapped around his cock, she nodded.

He tapped her cheek. "I'm not sure there's

room in your sweet mouth."

She moaned in entreaty.

Shifting his stance over the couch, he pushed in farther, using more control now that he was going deep. Her eyes widened, but he kept going. Kept filling her until he felt the resistance at the back of her throat. He heard her deep breaths, the evidence of her focus. He moved to pull out, but she grasped the back of his thighs, her palms slippery from her perspiration and his. He rocked himself right there, holding the position far inside, his eyes rolling back at the sensation along his dick. Sparks of pleasure ran down his spine and into the base of his cock, but he wrenched himself away from her wet heat.

Now.

She was limp in his arms as he lifted her. He settled her over the arm of the couch so that her hands and face could rest on the seat cushion and her ass was exposed to him. She had less control this way, so when he touched two fingers to her swollen pussy, she cried out but didn't move. Could hardly push back against him at all, her toes digging into the plush carpet beneath them. The sight of her was breathtaking—glistening folds all open for him. Plump and wet and ready for him.

He retrieved the wineglass and set the curved lip right at the base of her ass, sending rivulets of liquid over the puckered hole and down the valley of her sex. The liquid looked black against the leather beneath her pussy. A few dark drops landed on the carpet, but he didn't give a shit. He leaned in. The first taste of her was wine alone before the undertones of her flavor peeked through. Her moans were a sensual accompaniment to the meal he made of her. His cock throbbed, desperate to replace his tongue, but he ignored it. He licked and sucked at her until every trace of the savory drink was gone and he was drawing more liquid from inside her.

His balls were drawn up tight, his cock aching. He stood and leaned over her, brushing the hair from her face.

"You ready, sweetheart?"

She whimpered.

He plunged inside her, swift and deep. Her cry was muffled by the leather. Driven and desperate, he pulled back before pushing inside. All his control evaporated, his mercy for her missing in action. He could only fuck her as hard as he needed to and hope she could take it.

She sobbed gently, her hands clenching at nothing beside her head. He changed his angle, pushing down where he knew she needed it. She came with a keening cry and a rush of warmth around his cock. *Again.* He didn't let up, didn't slow or change a goddamned thing—just let her climb the peak until she came with a broken sound and more liquid, more heat. He wanted to drain her, to use her up, to fuck her so long and so hard that she would never leave.

He spread the soft cheeks of her ass apart, admiring the view. The bud of her asshole, her lips open for him. *Every part of you.* He felt his hands clench, and he forced them to relax. He shut his eyes and let himself go, lost himself in the tight squeeze of her pussy, drowning in the helpless sounds she made. Her orgasm clamped down around his cock, and he froze, crying out hoarsely as he emptied himself inside her, as he gave it all to her. *Every part of me.*

He panted over her back, shuddering at the clenching aftershocks. With regret, he withdrew from her body and helped her up. He pulled her down onto the couch, cradling her body with his own while she caught her breath.

"I didn't hurt you, did I? Didn't go too far?"

She sounded drugged. "Let's do it like that every time."

His lips curved into a smile in the moments before sleep dragged him under.

Chapter Twelve

Erin

ERIN SET HER chin on Blake's chest, enjoying the coarse male hairs that tickled her and the fresh soap-musk scent of him. At some point since dinner, he had gently woken her. They'd stumbled into the bathroom before crashing into bed, together again.

It was time, though. Time to broach the subject that could end this. End her.

"You nervous?" she asked, referring to his upcoming teaching stint in the vaguest way possible.

He kept his eyes closed, but the restless shift of his limbs gave him away. "Why? Should I be?"

No, but she was. She believed he'd be amazing as a professor, and whatever happened with her class, she would deal. But this teaching job was his first step in the direction of living again. She wouldn't take that away from him. Wouldn't even risk it with her presence.

"You don't have to go through with it. If you don't want to."

He opened his eyes then. His expression was guarded. "No one will know we're together," he said flatly. "You don't have to worry that people would judge you for…"

Her stomach clenched. For sleeping with him, because he had scars on his face.

She turned into his chest so he wouldn't see the flash of emotion that caught her off guard. Her heart broke a little every time he put himself down like that. And yet he had valid reasons to believe the world would care about how he looked…because the world *did* care. Because his fiancée had broken up with him, because his parents had mourned him as if he had died instead of lived. Because his entire career following his father's footsteps as a senator had detonated before it even began. The world cared, and she wouldn't lie to him.

"You know I'm not ashamed of you." Her voice was muffled. It would be better to look him in the eye as she said it, but he might misread the sympathy there as pity. He'd already had his pride stripped from him. She'd never take what he had left.

"I'm a bad choice for you in every way, Erin,

but damned if I'm going to leave you alone."

She looked up again, feeling a sad smile touch her face. "I have to tell you something. I'm not going to graduate this semester."

His face darkened. "What the hell are you talking about?"

When he looked angry, the mangled skin stayed frozen while the other side of his face lowered. A strange effect but an apt analogy, because part of him *was* frozen in that place of pain and grief while the rest of him struggled to move on.

She stroked his temple—the smooth one, because the other would just make him self-conscious. "It's just not the right time. One more semester won't kill me."

He reined in his surprise. "Okay, explain it to me. What's not right about this time?"

"I won't have enough for tuition, for one thing. I usually do the installment plan, but I can't count on having enough. The hours at my new job aren't very regular."

He was silent a moment. Even when he spoke, his voice was deceptively quiet. "We've talked about this. I want to help you."

"You want to give me money for sex...and I refuse."

"Then come back to work for me."

"That would still be you giving me money. No."

"You cleaned my house before we started anything. It's not like the employment is contingent on you sleeping with me. I've never given you any trouble, have I? Never complained about your work."

"That's exactly it. Would you complain if you needed to, knowing that it would interfere with our relationship?"

He rolled his eyes. "This conversation is…it's driving me crazy. I don't want you to work for me, Erin. I want you to move in with me. Let me cover your last semester's tuition. It's not a big deal."

She stared at him in shock. They'd never discussed her living here. For a moment she allowed herself to imagine. The beautiful, comfortable home she could come back to at the end of a school day. Reading outside on the deck, watching the wooded land behind where deer were occasionally spotted. Climbing into bed with him every night.

God, she wanted that so much. But not like this.

"Absolutely not," she said.

"Why not?"

"Because it's not okay for you to take care of me this way. Once I've graduated and I have a regular job, then I'll consider moving in. And paying for my share of things."

"Jesus, Erin."

"That's not unreasonable. That's how people do things."

He shook his head. "I'm not your mother's employer. I'm not going to try and take advantage of you."

She jerked back, removing herself from him, allowing the air between them to cool her. "That's not fair. This isn't about her."

Though maybe it was a little about her—and not only because of Doug's father. There had been other families. Other men. Other times her mother came home with red-rimmed eyes and bruises on her wrists. So maybe this was about her mother, just a little. Men had taken advantage of her mother in a way that Blake never would, but she wasn't totally comfortable with living under a man's control.

Their relationship was already uneven, but not in the ways that he thought about. Not because she was beautiful and he was scarred, which was what he thought.

He was older. She was younger.

He came from a wealthy family with a legacy in politics.

She had recited a number to get a free lunch in school.

He was smart and accomplished—even if he currently lived in reclusion—and she was just another grad student. Paying her own way with him was important. So even when he sat up and took her hands in his, she fortified herself.

"Be with me," he said with a soft, pleading note in his voice, and she almost, *almost* broke at that. What more could she want than to be with him? No money or school or frowning disapproval of society to block them.

"I don't care how we work it out. I don't care about the money. Take it, I'll sign it all over to you. You'll own the house, and I can live here at your mercy."

She did smile then, at the silly idea of that. Of her as some heiress and him bowing at her feet. Yes, silly but also sweet, because she believed he really didn't care. But as much as she loved him, as much as she knew he did understand tragedy in this world, she knew that only the rich thought money didn't matter. He'd never had to urge his mother to call the cops only to have her mother explain that if she made a fuss, any other jobs in town would go away. Even if he would never abuse it, she couldn't give him that kind of power over her.

"There's another reason I can't graduate this semester."

"Tell me." He squeezed her hands in his, comforting her even as she pushed him away.

"Remember I told you I needed one class aside from my thesis?" When he nodded, she continued, "Well, one of them didn't have a professor listed when I enrolled. It's happened before. Sometimes things aren't finalized early on and they fill it in later. So when I went to the bookstore, I saw they'd filled in the name of the professor. Someone new."

He stared at her. "No."

"Yeah. It was you. I guess it makes sense...a senior-level discussion course. I should have put it together sooner, but I thought you were going to teach ancient history."

"I looked at the student roster. There was no Erin."

"Erendira," she said, feeling shy. She had been naked with him a hundred ways, but he didn't know her real name. "No one could ever pronounce it. Not even the teachers in elementary school. And it just made me feel different from everyone."

"Erendira," he said, tasting the word. It sounded sweet on his lips.

"It means princess. My mom is something of a romantic."

He shook his head. "You don't have to postpone your graduation. I'll quit."

"You can't! You said yourself they need you to teach this course. If they have to cancel it, I still won't be able to graduate this semester and neither will the other students taking it."

"Shit," he said.

At that, she smiled. He didn't swear too often, so she knew he was almost speechless for him to do it twice in a row. "It's okay. I don't mind. I'm just happy you're going out there, finding your rightful place. That's more important than the exact date I graduate."

"It's more than that, Erendira. You've worked so much for this. I've seen how hard you've worked, both studying and cleaning my house so you can afford tuition."

"Erin," she corrected him softly. "And I can wait."

"And what are we going to do, put our relationship on hold for a year so you can graduate and pay your way with me? No," he said as if that decided it, and maybe it did. He was forceful that way, and she was…well, she was so disappointed not to graduate on time.

"You know it's not allowed."

He shrugged. "Probably not, but we already decided not to tell anyone. It's nobody's business but ours. I can teach the class, and you can take it."

She gave him a skeptical look. "I'm surprised you'd be okay with this."

"I'm not comfortable with it. But I'm committed to do this, and I'm sure as hell not going to let you put your life on hold for my sake. The rules are designed to protect people from being harassed, but that's not the case here."

A grin tipped her lips. "You don't feel even a little harassed? I mean, I did have sex with you in your office."

He pulled her onto his lap and kissed her. His lips moved against her as he murmured, "Now that can't happen again."

"Reason enough for us to call this whole thing off. Because that was crazy hot."

He rolled them over so that he straddled her. Her hands were pinned by his, her body trapped. And God, her sex tightened.

"I think I can find a substitute," he muttered, sliding down and spreading her legs wide.

"Oh God," she gasped. Then she gathered herself enough to purr, "Oh, Professor Morris."

He groaned. "You can't call me that in the classroom or I'll…"

"Or you'll what?"

"You might not like what happens." He set his lips to her sex and proceeded to make her like it very much indeed. She flung her head against the pillow, submerged with the pleasure, out of breath with it until all she could chant was his name. No games and no barriers. *Oh, Blake.*

She loved what happened with him. Every time, every way. On the outside he was a somber man, dark and serious. Brooding. All he needed was a fire-charred manor or windy cliffs to complete the picture. But the man within was so very different…so much lighter. He played with her, he laughed. He teased her to the brink of endurance and then gave her more than she'd imagined.

Even now he found a way to make this new. His tongue against her clit—as if it could ever get old. But this wasn't like the time before or the one before that. He nipped at the inside of her thighs and then soothed her with a luscious lick to her reddened skin. He swiped at the slick lips of her sex—so quickly she'd think he hadn't done it at all, until the shock and pleasure ran up her spine.

"No more teasing," she gasped.

"Are you sure? I think you like the teasing."

"I can't. I can't."

Two fingers inside her, homed directly on the spot, and it was too much. Far too much, so she arched herself up, crying out, "Wait. Stop."

"Well, which is it? Should I stop or make you come?"

"Please, Blake."

She heard his breath catch. When he spoke, his voice had fallen two octaves. "*Yes.* Again."

"Blake." Her mind was a blur, at the center of a tornado and watching the storm swirl around her. She couldn't have moved, and God, she didn't want to. He was the calm and the storm all at once, both peaceful and tragic, both beautiful in their own way. "Please."

"Say it again," he said, and she couldn't remember what he wanted.

"More. Yes," she babbled. "Blake."

He pushed her knees up and back with both hands. "Say *Please, Blake.*"

She was unable to move like this, with her bent legs tucked against her chest, bound by the tight constraints of her own body and his unyielding hands on her knees.

"Please." She swallowed. "Blake."

"Again."

She sobbed softly. "Please, Blake."

Without removing his hands from her legs, he lined up his cock. The head felt impossibly broad and she so exposed. In a smooth thrust, he pushed inside. He gave her exactly what she wanted, as he always would. Whether in bed or in life, whether her body or her heart, she could always trust in him to fulfill her. It poured into her, his love and admiration, leaving only a little room for doubts. A very small place where she hoped she was doing the same good for him.

Chapter Thirteen

Blake

BLAKE LOOKED OVER his lecture notes. Again. He already knew the outline forwards and backwards. He could theorize and expound for hours on every point listed—and had done so, in email exchanges and phone calls with old friends and a few new ones in his seclusion since the explosion. He knew the nuances of the material, he felt passionately about the real-life impact. In Erin's slang, he had this on lock.

But he couldn't shake the disquiet. That fear he was making a mistake. The fear that it would all blow up in his face, though that had already happened—literally. What could be worse than the pain of first-degree burns and losing his teammates in a single blast? Of having his fiancée break things off when he returned home and losing the ability to follow in his father's footsteps as a senator?

All he had to do now was stand in front of

thirty grad students and ignore the way their gazes would nervously dart away from his face. The small classroom had a single large table with chairs gathered around and cluttered into the corners. A desk was at the front, but the whole effect was intimate. Perfect for the discussions that were common in advanced graduate classes. A little too close for comfort, considering.

Maybe his nerves had more to do with a certain student in particular.

God, Erin. He was crazy about her. She needed this class and he needed this job—this chance to re-enter society on a temporary, part-time basis. He'd looked up the university bylaws to be certain, and surprisingly there was no specific language forbidding it. Still, he assumed the clause on professional behavior would preclude everything he did to her sweet body each night. And again, the next morning.

Fuck.

He should quit. Confess a conflict of interest to the dean and walk out. And leave them hanging with no one to teach this course... It was professional suicide. He'd get blacklisted from every university in the country. Not to mention all the students whose schedules and graduation plans would go haywire if this class fell through.

Including Erin. But if something went wrong…

He stood. He'd quit and deal with things how he always did—head-on. Anything was better than jeopardizing his relationship with her.

The papers slid haphazardly onto the chipped rosewood desk as he stood. Determined now, he stuffed the whole bundle into his briefcase. His loafers whispered on the scuffed hardwood floors. He swung open the ancient heavy door and almost ran directly into Melinda.

Melinda, the woman he'd once loved. The fiancée who had dumped him when she saw his face and realized he'd never live up to the promise of public service. The person who'd gone into his house that night and made herself at home. He did not have time for this shit, and he almost brushed past her and kept walking. But then he remembered Erin's face when she'd seen Melinda at his house. Erin had been hurt by her asshole boyfriend before, but anyone would be concerned about the situation. Melinda had been his fiancée, for God's sake, and she was suddenly showing up in his home? He had to nip this in the bud.

Frustrated, he practically growled, "Come in. Close the door before anyone gets here."

She smiled, her lids lowering. "Whatever you say, Blake. I always liked it when you gave me orders."

He shook his head. "It's not like that, Melinda. You and I are done, exactly how I told you when you came to my office. I thought you understood then, but apparently not. What the hell were you thinking breaking into my house?"

She pouted. "I had my old key. Anyway, I realized I made a mistake letting you go." Her voice dropped, the same way he'd always found so damn sexy. Now he felt nothing but impatience and annoyance.

"So, telling me I could never be the man you'd once loved…that was a mistake?"

She threw up her hands. "I didn't know how to deal with it. It was hard, okay?"

He felt a stirring of sympathy. The whole situation had been a fucking mess. He didn't want to judge her too harshly for bailing. He knew very well what the explosion had ruined, and it was a lot more than his face. But that didn't mean they could turn back the clock. He wouldn't even want to.

"It's over between us. I've moved on."

Her eyes narrowed. "So there *is* another woman."

Annoyance clawed at him. "I don't care what you tell yourself about this. You can paint me as the monster. Lord knows I already look the part. But we're not doing this anymore. I've had the locks changed. If you show up again, I'm calling the cops."

Her eyes widened, nostrils flared. At least he'd finally made his point.

"Fine," she ground out. "I was only doing this to be nice. You're pathetic anyway, walking around campus with no shame. Don't you realize everyone is staring at you?"

Unfortunately, he did. "We're done here."

She gave him a sly smile. "What am I even talking about? No one would date you now unless you paid them. I'm only here because your mother called me, worried about her little boy."

Jesus. Dear old mom had never given up on him like his father had.

"Are you finished?"

"I'll see you at the faculty ball. You wouldn't miss it, would you?" Her smirk made it clear she expected him to hide.

"Of course not."

The gleam in her eyes was bloodthirsty. "I look forward to it."

"As do I."

After she left, he let his eyes shut, a small release of his frustration. At least that part was over. The side of his face burned with the familiar, daily pain—and a small but real dose of humiliation. *Walking around campus with no shame.*

Footsteps approached. It was too late to back down now. Hell, it had already been too late. With a sinking feeling, he stepped back as two students burst in. They were clearly in the middle of a conversation, one animating her words with her hands, the other with his head down, looking at his phone as he walked. The girl saw him first. She stopped. And gawked. The boy glanced at her first, mouth open mid-sentence. Then he saw Blake and his mouth gaped open.

Blake tried to clear the air. "I'm Professor Morris. I'll be teaching this course. Grab a seat, we'll get started in a minute."

He found a smile, the one that used to put people at ease. His world had been divided into before and after. Before, he could charm anyone with that smile. Now, he knew, it looked more like a grimace. The boy seemed to recover better. He brushed it off with a nod of greeting before hitching his backpack and grabbing a seat. The girl took it a little harder, peering at his face as if it were a puzzle for her to solve. Blake forced the smile to stay in place and gritted his teeth. She finally turned to take a seat beside her friend when Erin walked in.

All the air sucked out of the room, like it always did when Erin was near. The explosion had brought him low, but it was nothing compared to what she did to him. The scars were a frustration, the constant pain a prolonged sort of torture. But the pain she could deliver would devastate him.

And she wasn't looking at him.

Her head was down as she passed him, leaving only the sweet Erin scent in her wake. She took the seat farthest in the back, though the room was small enough that they were still close. Even as she unpacked a notebook and pen, she consistently avoided eye contact.

He frowned. They'd agreed not to give away their relationship, but this was extreme. It probably hinted at inappropriate behavior more than outright flirting would have done. No, it was more than circumspection. Something was wrong. And he'd have to sit through a whole class before he could ask her what it was.

ERIN

ERIN FOCUSED ON lining up her pens beside the notebook.

She flipped the page open to a fresh one. Wrote her name in careful script.

Okay, she was stalling. Because Blake was looking at her curiously and she couldn't face him at this exact moment, not with the other students between them. His stare was a force pulling her toward him, a question she felt compelled to answer. Finally a new student entered, and he turned his attention away. She felt a corresponding chill at the loss.

She'd practically sprinted from meeting with her advisor, hoping she could make it here before anyone else and wish Blake luck. She'd skidded to a halt, out of breath, when she heard Professor Jenkins's voice inside with him. It had sounded, in that smattering of words, as if she'd asked him to the faculty ball. And he'd accepted.

Even though she knew he wouldn't do that to her.

Finding them together, she'd flashed back to that night she'd seen the woman at Blake's house. And gotten a resurgence of that same old anger. Even after Professor Jenkins had stormed out, looking pretty angry in her own right, Erin had remained in the hallway. She didn't want him to see her this way. She trusted that when she heard the full story, everything would be fine. But in the meantime, all she felt was sad.

Only when two other students went inside had she been able to stroll inside and pretend indifference.

Someone took the seat next to her. She glanced up. A smiling face.

"I didn't know you'd be here," he said. "Good to see a familiar face, though."

She smiled. "Jeremy. Didn't I see you outside Dr. Miller's office?"

"I meant to catch you after, but you left so quickly."

She blushed, thinking of exactly who she'd been in such a rush to see. "Didn't want to be late. First day and all."

"What's the deal with this guy?" he asked, and it took her a minute to register he was talking about Blake. *Professor Morris*, she reminded herself.

"What about him?"

"His face, for one thing." When she scowled, he quickly continued. "And where did he come from? This is an advanced-level class. I can't believe they gave it to a new adjunct professor."

"It probably means they have a lot of faith in him." The defensiveness surprised her. She'd have to watch that if she didn't want people guessing they had something going on.

Jeremy looked at her speculatively. "Sure. Whatever." He pulled out a laptop and plugged it into the wall behind them. "Besides, only one more semester and I'm out of here."

She grinned. Now that she could relate to. "Me too."

"Man, I can't wait. I'm so done with this place."

She was right there with him. With her degree, she would finally be able to support herself on more than loans. She'd finally be able to afford more than a shared, crappy apartment. Could she really blame Blake for speaking to Professor Jenkins or wanting to see her outside of work hours? She was his equal. Erin wanted that too.

She sneaked a glance at him. He'd gone back to his desk and opened his briefcase. The papers inside looked crumpled and disorganized. That was unlike him.

Distantly a buzz signaled the start of class. The newer buildings didn't have bells, but this was one of the more historical buildings on campus, which meant the furniture was all scratched up and the A/C was constantly on the fritz. The low hum of conversation fell into silent expectation. Blake set down the papers and came around the desk empty-handed. He turned one of the chairs around and straddled it.

In a way, meeting them all as equals.

Her heart softened. It must have been hard for him to face everyone on the same level, without the shield or props that most professors used, even ones without scars. But he wasn't showing any nervousness. He looked calm, competent. Like an experienced professor instead of a man who'd been ripped apart, physically and emotionally. Like a soldier.

He introduced himself as *Professor Morris but call me Blake*. She smiled at that. He'd said something similar to her at the beginning when she'd showed up to clean his house, though it had been *Mr. Morris*. Back then, she'd instinctively resisted, recognizing that intimacy between them could grow like wildfire. So he was always Mr. Morris to her...until they'd slept together.

Now he was Blake.

He spoke with a smooth baritone, easy to hear and understand as he went over the tenets of the class, the schedule and the research paper that would account for the bulk of their grade. Everyone, including Erin, scribbled down the information.

"Okay, let's get down to business. I'm told the

class textbook was listed with the enrollment information."

She'd been the one to tell him that. In his day, they'd only gotten that information on the first day of class. That was how he'd said it too—*in my day*. She had laughed. As if he was ancient instead of fifteen years older.

She pulled out her textbook along with the rest of the class. The books lay in a circle on the table, unopened.

He paused for a moment, as if thinking.

"This isn't an issues class. I do expect you to stay up-to-date with what's happening in the political sphere...and catch yourself up if for some reason you haven't been following the news for the past five years. But I'm not going to tell you how to feel about euthanasia or whether you should support a candidate who smoked pot. That's your job to figure out, as a citizen and as esteemed graduates of this program. This class is about giving you the means to convey those feelings and your support. The language. The tools."

Another pause, and in any other class, there would be shuffling as students turned, disinterested, to their phones. Instead, there was only thoughtful silence. Erin found herself thinking as well. What tools did she have? Responsibility as a citizen…those were strong words, but he said them without rancor or judgment. With a certain sense of trust, as if he believed that a bunch of hungover college students really would come up with the right answers on their own.

"What's your name?" he asked one of the boys across from her.

"Uh, Allen."

"Allen, can you read the first paragraph of the first chapter, please?"

Pages rustled as everyone flipped open to the right page. The chapter heading said, *PRECEDENT*.

Allen read aloud, "A precedent is an earlier event or action regarded as an example or guide to be considered in similar circumstances or a principle established in a previous situation that may be applied to subsequent cases with similar circumstances."

"Hmm," Blake said. "That's a perfectly whitewashed definition, but I think we can do better than that. Anyone want to give it a try?"

The room was quiet. Blake waited.

Finally Jeremy spoke up from beside her. "It's a way of explaining current behavior based on something that happened in the past."

"Excellent. Framing the present using the

past. What's the benefit of doing this?"

"If something was true then, then it holds that it will be true again," another student supplied.

"Using the past as context. Good."

"Consistency," a surly-faced boy said. "Rules are established and then followed."

"Yes. Right. What else?" When no one answered, he continued, "Why is precedent such an important tool that they put it front and center, first chapter in the textbook?"

Erin looked down at the glossy white pages with stark-black ink. A few sentences had been highlighted from the previous owner. There was a lot of small text but nothing to give her a clue as to why this was first—or even important at all.

Blake seemed to settle in, resting his elbows on the chair back in front of him.

"There was a time that no one could match the power of Rome," he began. "One who came close was Carthage, with its advantageous trade position and well-developed culture. Unfortunately, the Romans considered the Carthaginians to be savages and a threat to their way of life. Or so they claimed. In truth they simply wanted the wealth of Carthage. So, following an inspection of the city and surrounding countryside, a Roman commission reported to the Senate 'an abundance of ship-building materials' and claimed the Carthaginians had built up their fleet in violation of the treaty."

Blake paused his story and reached back to take a sip of water. That moment of quiet seemed to give the girl across from Erin courage.

"You're slanting it," she blurted out. As thirty faces turned to her, she blushed, looking like she wanted to take it back.

Blake turned to her too, unoffended. "How so?" he asked mildly.

"You're telling us their motivations, that the Romans really just wanted their wealth, but you don't know that. Maybe they believed the other people were a threat."

"Maybe so. And that's a benefit of history, we can look inside their private writings and their memoirs. We can get a firmer grasp of what they thought outside their public speeches. Unlike current events, where all we have is the public view."

"Another benefit of precedent," Erin said under her breath.

He flashed her a quick smile. "Yes. Exactly. Now the Carthaginians knew they were going to get their asses handed to them." One of the boys snickered at the language here. Blake continued.

"So they pleaded with the Senate, swearing that they were not in violation of the treaty, promising that they would surrender without a fight.

"So the clever Romans came up with three challenges. On the first, they requested three hundred sons from the noble families as captives. Carthage sent them over in a ship. For the second challenge, they demanded that Carthage send them armor and weaponry. Carthage complied. When it came time for the final challenge, the diplomat explained to the Carthaginians that they would need to move their city, the buildings, everything, ten miles to the left."

Someone snorted. "Why?"

"The location near the sea had corrupted Carthage's temperament," Blake said. "At least according to the commissioner."

Quiet laughs of disbelief rang out in the small room. It was ridiculous, and yet it was real. History.

"Here Carthage had no choice but to refuse. Imagine moving a whole infrastructure ten miles to the left. It was impossible. Clearly Rome was looking for an excuse to invade and steal their resources."

"Bullshit," said the boy who'd spoken earlier, the one whose face seemed set in a perpetual frown. He was large too, bulky but also intimidating. The chair and table they used looked too small for him.

"Sorry?" Blake asked casually.

"I said it's bullshit. You said you aren't here to tell us what to think, but you're doing just that."

"Do you disagree with my representation of the Third Punic War?" he inquired.

The boy made a rude sound. "You aren't talking about any Punic War or the Romans, and we all know it."

"Then who am I talking about?"

"You're talking about the Iraq War. About Bush. This is some liberal propaganda."

"It's just a story. Why does it have to mean anything?"

"Because—" The boy broke off. He snorted softly. "Because it's a goddamn precedent."

Blake hummed in agreement and approval. "Precedent is useful for a lot of reasons, but stories are how we connect with the world, how we understand the bigger picture. I told a story about Rome, and you naturally connected that to Iraq. There's power in stories. Never underestimate that."

He directed their attention back to the textbook, but Erin felt much more interested in these theoretical words now that she understood the application. Everyone seemed to join in with enthusiasm, even the boy who had challenged Blake before. Any animosity had faded under the strength of curiosity…and the power of stories.

No, she wouldn't likely underestimate that again. Nor would she underestimate him again. He may have been reluctant to accept the job, but once here, he would have no reservations about performing to his fullest. And his fullest was very, very good.

If she hadn't known him before, she was pretty sure she'd have a major crush on her professor at this point. But she had known him before, had seen him joyous and brought low. She'd seen him laugh with abandon and climax with an agonized groan. Her feelings right now transcended a crush. They soared into love.

CHAPTER FOURTEEN

ERIN

ERIN SPENT HER days in class or in the library working on her research paper. Her nights were always spent in the same place—Blake's arms. Sometimes in her apartment, but more often at his place so as to let her roommate sleep in peace. Courtney never mentioned the noise except to keep a running tally on the whiteboard in the kitchen of how long it had been since she'd gotten laid.

The two summer sessions were highly abbreviated. Instead of meeting twice a week for a whole semester, they met every day for six weeks. The next thing Erin knew they were halfway through. Halfway to her goal and completely, head over heels in love with Blake.

She'd been worried about him being her professor—more than she'd let on to him or Courtney. But he was respectful and considerate to all his students, and she was eager to learn from him. Everything was almost perfect. Almost, because they still had to keep things a secret. That night, she drove to his place.

She wanted to throw her arms around him when he opened the door. His grin was mischievous, holding both a question for her and pride at a job well done. Instead she settled for a huge smile in return. She couldn't have held it back anyway. He'd been amazing in class, authoritative and relatable as usual.

"You were fantastic. I knew you would be, but damn. You even surpassed what I was thinking."

He shut the door as she passed. "No one ran away screaming, so I'm calling it a win."

She rolled her eyes. "No one even notices how you look anymore."

Though she noticed how he looked now, still wearing his slacks and dress shirt, though he'd rolled the sleeves up. His clothes were a little rumpled, his hair a little mussed. Her hungry gaze roamed his body, and when she met his eyes, the desire in them matched her own.

He pressed her against the wall. His kiss said it wasn't a good time for discussion. It demanded things of her, things like submission and sweetness, like passion and playfulness, and she was too happy to oblige. His tongue darted into her mouth and then out again, quicksilver, and she was left to chase into his with her own.

His hand cupped her neck, a solid and comforting touch that morphed into something dirtier as he grasped her hair. She gasped at the sensation. Her cunt clenched in time with his fist. His other hand slid up from her waist, underneath her shirt, the hot contact enough to melt her into the implacable surface behind her.

He broke the kiss but continued to touch her, everywhere, as if it had been months or years instead of hours and days.

"It's harder than I expected." He nibbled a path down her neck.

Oh God, that felt good. Her hips bucked. "Teaching the class?"

"Pretending I don't know you."

Her heart squeezed. "For me too. But I'm proud every time I see you there."

His smile was almost boyish. She had a hard time even seeing the scarring as some specific impediment. It was just the way he looked—a part of him. The only reason she regretted it was because she knew it gave him pain.

He would occasionally turn away and grit his teeth. It came and went, he said, like being burned all over again, echoes of the past. She would have done anything to take that away if she could. She loved, loved, loved him. And he loved her back, she was sure of it. So this insecurity business could die an ugly death, as far as she was concerned. No reason to hold him accountable just because some guy had been a jerk her sophomore year.

"I need to tell you something," she said. He raised an eyebrow, and she continued. "I heard the tail end of your conversation with Professor Jenkins. The first day of class."

"Shit." He shut his eyes. "I'm sorry. I hoped you wouldn't see her there. Erin, I swear I didn't—"

"No, it's okay. You don't have to explain. I trust you, and I understand that she might come speak to you once in a while. You guys do share an employer, at least for the semester. So I didn't want you to have to worry that I'm going to freak out if you have a conversation. I wouldn't even have said anything, except I don't want you to feel like you have to hide from me."

He pulled her to the couch. "I appreciate your progressive views on the matter, but as our fellow classmate would say, bullshit."

She blinked. "What?"

"You have every right to be upset about finding me like that or at the very least to know what we talked about. And even if you don't insist on it, I want to tell you. I made it clear to her that we were over. I told her if she came to my house again, that I'd call the cops on her."

"You actually said that?"

He shrugged. "It's the truth. What she did was beyond inappropriate, and I needed to nip it in the bud. For my relationship with you but also for myself. I can't promise she'll never do anything again, but I have no interest in her. None. And I'm pretty sure I pissed her off enough where she'll want nothing to do with me."

She arched a brow. "Setting a precedent, are we?"

He chuckled. "You're going to throw all my lectures back at me, aren't you?"

"Most likely. Why, you going to get fed up with me?"

"Never." Another kiss, softer this time. "Stay with me." A press of his lips to hers. "Wrapped up so tight I never have to worry that I'll wake up and you won't be there."

As if to obey him, her limbs moved without thought, her arms twining around his neck, her legs hitching around his thighs. Her back arched up from the wall, seeking the hard length and hot pulse of him, trying to connect them everywhere.

"I'll never leave you," she whispered.

She felt him through her jeans, felt his cock jump in response to her words. They were connected, the emotions and the sex. They tangled together like their bodies and hearts, not elegant but instead grasping, pleading, begging. Needing.

She shuddered, silently beseeching, but when her tongue found the heavy beat at his neck, she moaned. He tasted like musk and man, like faith and irreverence all at once. His skin here was unmarred, uninjured, and yet still rough. The uneven rasp of a healthy, vibrant man who had worked and fought and weathered the world before finding refuge in her arms.

He reacted to the wet slide of her tongue violently. He bucked against her, slamming her into the wall.

"Wait," he muttered. "One minute…just."

She didn't want to wait. Didn't want him to bring himself under control, burying the passion somewhere deep and unreachable. She grazed his collarbone with her teeth, an animal instinct to incite and distract him. To draw out the beast inside him—not the wounded skin he thought made him so, but the hard, angry part of him.

The part he kept carefully away from her, treating her instead like fragile glass. As if she wouldn't be able to handle him—or as if she wouldn't want to. She couldn't blame him after the way Professor Jenkins had left him at his most vulnerable. He'd learned to hide his pain and frustration. He'd learned to doubt Erin too. But she was stronger than that. She wasn't delicate nor easily bruised. And she was greedy. Nothing but the whole of him would be good enough.

She slid her hand down the plane of his chest and abs, down to the cloth-covered cock below. It strained against his pants, restricted by clothes and by him. *However she wants it, don't push too far.* That was fine at the beginning, but not now. She had something to prove and maybe so did he.

She squeezed gently, luxuriating in the stuttered breaths bellowing from his chest, the low, pained grunt emanating from his throat, and, God, his hands—the way they pushed like beams against the wall on either side of her head, straining with the force of his lust and yet holding steady to allow her to explore. So much strength, so much restraint. He was a lashing storm clasped tightly in a steel box, and she held the key.

With her fingers flying, she unbuckled his belt and took out his cock. It fell heavily into her palm, burning up against her skin. She fell to her knees and tongued him, kissed him with all the force and passion that she had given his mouth just seconds earlier. She had sucked a man before, had even done this to him before, but never quite like this. Like making out with his cock, like making love to him with her mouth. He was smooth and slippery on her tongue, the faint salt barely registering beneath the passion that drove her. And to her delight, he was too caught up in the moment to censor himself. He dropped one hand and clasped her head, thrusting deep in beautiful rhythm. This was no careful role-play like they had done in his office that day, this was unruly and wild, a deluge of sex and sensation.

He pulled away—jerked himself back from her, panting. "God, Erin. God."

She sank back to the wall, the slab cool against her fevered skin. The air felt thick and sumptuous, hard to breathe but nourishing too.

"How do you want me?" she asked, her voice low.

"I'm too far gone after... I'm on the edge, Erin. Let me step back and then I'll make this good for you."

"I don't want you to make it good for me. I want you to jump."

She reached for him, tugging the pants that hung at his thighs, down his legs and off completely, leaving him bared in only a dress shirt hung open. The lines of his body curved so elegantly, all that power contained, the strength sharply forged—exactly like the man within. She stroked down the outside of his calf, the tanned skin and sprinkling of male hair, admiring.

When she looked up, the question was in her eyes—the plea. *Please?* He groaned, and it sounded so dire, like something had perished, and she hoped it was his self-control.

He pointed to the living room where the hardwood floor softened to plush carpet. "Hands and knees."

She scrambled to comply, dropping her clothes as she went, shedding out of them like finding a new skin—this one molten and pure. Nothing but sex and sensuality. Only helpless, guileless intimacy here. The carpet felt scratchy on her forearms, a metal scrub brush on ceramic. She turned back, offering herself up to him, letting the embarrassment wash over her and heighten the gift of herself.

BLAKE

BLAKE TOOK HIS time retrieving a condom from his pants pocket, slipping it over the length of his cock. Not looking at her—he couldn't. Like Erin had done in class that first day with her pens and her notebook, keeping herself hidden because to see would be too much. Her beauty too blinding and his own weakness at the fore. He wanted to ravage her in a way that would change her, indelibly bind her to him so that neither of them could break loose.

He was afraid, though, of the tension rippling through his arms, the dark murmurs of his heart. He could be too rough like this. He needed to check himself even if she wanted to give him full rein. What if he hurt her? What if he scared her away?

But he wasn't sure he could stop himself. Just warning himself to be careful wasn't enough, not when his whole body bristled to take her. Erin knelt before him, the curve of her ass so sweet, the pink lips of her sex glistening. He was ravenous for her, desperate to be inside her and over her, surround her until all she breathed was him.

Be careful, he admonished himself. *Go slow.*

He fisted his cock and forced himself to speak evenly. "What are you thinking about? Right now."

Her eyes widened. "About you. How you'll feel inside me."

"You need to come?"

"Yes," she breathed.

"When's the last time you got yourself off?"

She blinked. If he wasn't mistaken, a blush spread over her cheeks, spilling over the back of her shoulders. "You mean the last time we…?"

"Not me. You. How long has it been since you touched yourself?"

She turned her face into the carpet, muffling her answer. "This morning."

He stroked up the inside of her thigh, not wanting her to feel alone in this and needing— needing to touch her soft skin. Not wanting to be alone in this either. Blood coursed hotly through his veins, pounding a beat of urgency and desire. Of possession, even though he knew that wasn't right. Wasn't good.

She deserved to be cherished, but all he could think was to hold her down and fuck her. She deserved to be worshipped, but he imagined his every sinful dream upon her body. Most of all, she deserved a better man, one whole and unbroken, but he would never let her go.

The silky skin at the top of her leg was already

damp. He drew circles there idly, needing to stall before he plunged into her. Before he hurt her. He would accept her submission, her trust. He'd use her sweet body and in doing so reach his own bliss. Selfish, monstrous—that was him.

He leaned down, murmuring the only love words he could think in the moment. "Show me. Make yourself come for me."

With a moan of acceptance, she reached down. He could see flashes of pale as her fingers worked quickly at her clit. Thick blinds filtered light from the evening, a shy illumination of her gorgeous curves and shadows beneath. He knelt behind her and bent his head. She tasted lovely. He reached deeper, nudging her legs farther apart and delving into her with his tongue. She shivered, and the motion of her hand sped up.

He'd directed this, but he felt strangely powerless. He could lick her, caress her with his tongue, but it was she who controlled the pace, she who stroked herself toward climax. It wasn't what he'd intended at the start, but her pleasure was its own sweet reward.

She began to rock in a familiar rhythm. He grabbed her hips to hold her steady. His harsh grip seemed to spur something inside her. Her sounds were frantic now, her fingers desperate. He slid his own two fingers into the warm clasp of her body, finding the right angle and perfect spot, meeting her caress with his tongue through her swollen flesh.

She cried out as she came, sounding desperate and so wholly his that he reared back and slammed inside her before she had finished. He pushed inside again and again, not letting her relax or find comfort in the fullness. It was different than ever before, and that thought only spurred him higher. Harder. Deeper inside until she clenched around him in a bid for reprieve.

He couldn't, though. Couldn't stop, couldn't breathe. *More, more.* He slid a palm along the sweat-slicked skin of her back and grasped her hair at the base. He pulled her up against him so she knelt upright and him behind her, almost beneath her, fucking upward. Reaching around her, he found her clit and fondled it with the same rhythm she'd used on herself, having learned her secrets now.

She gasped and sobbed in his embrace, hands damp with her own desire, clinging to his arms and scrabbling at his sides—wherever she could reach, which wasn't much. He had her in hand now, under his control in a way he both loathed and craved. He wanted to give her all his gentleness only to find there was none left. He sucked at her neck, leaving marks for the world and for her—but mostly for himself. To know that she was his and to never doubt, never fear.

Still holding her steady with his hand tangled in her hair. Still circling her clit in time with the pulse of her cunt around his cock. "Come," he murmured in her ear. "Come for me."

"I can't."

"Do it now."

He pinched her clit, and she came with a hoarse cry. Her pussy squeezed him tight. He almost came—*not yet, almost.*

"Again," he demanded.

"No more. Oh God, I really can't."

But she could. Her inner muscles still rippled around him, her last climax hardly faded.

He bit her earlobe gently. "I want to feel you come again. I want that sweet pussy to squeeze me until I can't hold back anymore. I want to feel your wetness drip down my cock to my balls. Can you do that for me, sweetheart?"

She might have cried out his name, but the sound muffled in his ears as she did just what he'd ordered. As she came and shook in his arms while her sex tightened almost painfully around his cock. His vision went white, his body rigid. He came in a moment of blinding ecstasy and helpless, heartless need. With a cry of despair and release. With the knowledge that he would never survive it if she left him too.

He curled onto his side, catching her as she fell, panting. "Sorry, sorry, sorry."

"No." Her voice was raw. "Don't you dare say you're sorry. Don't you dare."

So he didn't say it aloud, he just thought it. *I'm sorry, but I can't let you go. You're mine now, God help you.*

CHAPTER FIFTEEN

ERIN

ERIN STRETCHED. HER muscles felt wrung out and used well.

She turned her head, facing her lover with a lazy smile. Blake had his eyes closed, arm slung over his face. He grew less bold in the aftermath, as if she might find his scars ugly without the haze of arousal to soften him. He had also maneuvered them so that she saw his unmarred side. He did that constantly, so smoothly she hardly noticed until after. She wasn't sure he even knew he did it. The burned skin was only a glimpse on the opposite cheek. Shiny tissue. White and pink that didn't tan to bronze with the rest of his skin.

She wished she could tell him it didn't matter. But that wasn't really true. How many people wore the darkest part of them on their faces? What a different world it would be if we walked around with signs that proclaimed the worst thing that had happened to us.

For her mother, it would be whatever had happened in the house where she'd worked as a maid and then suddenly hadn't anymore. For Erin, it would be when her boyfriend had taken her to meet his parents and they realized his father had been the one to hurt her mother. When her boyfriend had called later with that bullshit story about her mom stealing from them, sure that his father was innocent of any wrongdoing. When he'd left her to find her own ride back to campus and when she'd seen him walking between buildings with another girl on his arm. *Broken spirit*, her mother's sign would say. *Broken heart* for Erin.

Broken body for Blake.

Put that way, she felt lucky. Everyone had pain in their pasts. Some had it worse than others, but no one was untouched. The difference was that Blake was introduced that way. The rest of them had their smooth-skinned shells to hide behind.

He turned to face her, exposing himself. She looked into his eyes and felt herself fall into them—the contentment there and the shame.

"What are you thinking about?" he murmured.

She almost smiled at the echo of his earlier

words. During sex he'd asked that question. And her answer was the same, in essence. "About you."

He raised a brow. "Anything in particular?"

She studied the smooth bronze of his skin, the mottled pink. The courage with which he faced each day, holding that damned sign up, his head held high.

"How beautiful you are."

Something flickered in his eyes. "That's cruel," he said mildly.

She flinched. "I mean it. You're beautiful to me."

He faced the ceiling again. "Fuck, Erin. I never asked you to lie to me."

She propped herself on her elbow. "Why do you think I have sex with you if I don't find you attractive?"

"Pity?" he said, so cavalierly she knew he was baiting her.

And it worked, damn him. "Then why do you have sex with me?" she challenged.

He was still a moment. His expression impassive, he turned his head and gave her a long, slow perusal from her wild, disheveled hair down her naked body to where her toes were tucked under the sheet. He caressed her breast, running his thumb down the side, the rough pad of his finger like fine sandpaper on her sensitive skin.

His hand remained on her breast, a soft weight, a link between them as he looked her in the eye. "I love you, Erin. I'm not sure it's enough. In fact, I know it's not, but I can't keep myself away from you. It has nothing to do with the fact that you're the most beautiful woman I've ever seen."

She swallowed thickly. For someone declaring his love and her beauty, he didn't seem happy about it. "Is it a problem?"

He smiled slightly. His voice was hoarse. "No. Not right now."

A chill climbed up her spine. Only then could she see the risk he'd taken, teaching a class where she would be a student. At first he'd resisted because he didn't want to rejoin society, didn't want to work again and walk among the living, preferring the sanctuary he had made for himself in this house.

They would make it work with him as her professor, limiting the moral dilemma as best they could. She would do her best, which usually earned her an A or the rare B. Both were commonly the only grades given in the small advanced master's courses, the idea being that all the C and D students had been weeded out by then anyway.

But he would grade her fairly, regardless. He was too honorable to do anything else.

More than the potential for conflict between them, what if they were found out? Would there be some sort of inquisition? Would he be fired with a scandal on his virtual resume? Of course no one would find out. And she wouldn't let the grade come between them, whatever it ended up being. But there was an awful lot of room for error in this plan. He must have known that, and he'd accepted it without complaint.

For her.

"Let's keep it that way," she said, brushing back the hair from his forehead. She pet him, her large, sedated cat, until his eyes stayed shut and his breathing evened out. He slept, but she continued to caress him, needing the contact.

How could she have been so reckless with him—with his career and his life? And how had he let her do that? Though he wasn't confrontational by nature, preferring diplomacy to a direct conflict, he knew how to stand up to people. It was how he'd isolated himself so completely, how he'd avoided getting sucked back into the world despite repeated calls from the dean, from his parents. He'd laid down the facts with Melinda, threatening to call the police if she pulled any more stunts here. But she'd simply asked him, *here, do this thing*, and he'd nodded and done it. A heady sort of power, but one she could misuse by accident if she wasn't careful.

ERIN

THIS MORNING HAD been another great class. The group had loosened up over the weeks, with the other students holding active discussions that sometimes spilled out into the hallway after class. Then Erin had spent the early afternoon in a small café right off campus, where she'd enjoyed a strawberry drink with tapioca pearls while going over her notes.

She packed up her books and headed back to the department offices. She had a standing weekly appointment with her advisor, Dr. Miller, to go over her progress and get feedback. The day was uncommonly warm. Sunlight winked at her from around the spires and cornices of the elaborate old buildings.

Her eyes were narrowed and downcast to avoid the bright light. She pushed through the double doors, blinking at the sudden dimness.

"There you are, Erin," a voice said. "I've been waiting for you."

At first she couldn't place it, but the sinking feeling was answer enough. Her vision cleared. Melinda was smiling at her. It wasn't a nice smile.

"Dr. Jenkins," she said in greeting, hoping the dismay didn't come through.

"Come into my office and we can talk."

"Oh. Well, I have a meeting with—"

"Not for a few minutes, right? You're always early. You can spare a few minutes for me."

She did have a few minutes until her meeting started, which she normally spent on the bench in the hallway, and Melinda seemed to know that. She didn't want to talk to her right now, especially blindsided like this. But she wasn't willing to make the leap to insubordination. And Melinda was technically on the committee. She followed the other woman down the hall and into her office.

When Erin was inside, Melinda shut the door. Erin hid her grimace. She supposed it would be a long talk then. She sat in one of the chairs in front of the desk, and Melinda crossed the room to take her seat.

"Now," Melinda said. "I took the liberty of looking at your transcript. Very impressive."

"Thank you."

"Especially for someone with your background. I really respect that." Melinda's tone made it clear she meant the exact opposite.

Erin gritted her teeth. How would the woman even *know* about her background? She'd been doing more digging than just her transcript.

Melinda continued. "I'm concerned about this. About you."

"What about me?"

"This idea you have about getting your master's degree. You realize it's not necessary for many positions."

No doubt she expected Erin to be a secretary. "I understand, but I want to do this." Not to mention she was already two years in and inches away from the finish line. "I believe it will help me achieve my long-term goals."

"Hmm. I've also had a look at your financial records. That's a large amount of debt, the loans that cover what the scholarship didn't. Is that really something you want to saddle yourself with so early in your career? You're very young."

Erin blinked. "Well, with all due respect, I've already taken on the debt. It's not something I could undo even if I wanted to, at this point."

"Really?" A thin, well-shaped eyebrow arched. "There are ways that pretty students sometimes relieve themselves of such a burden. A rich benefactor, for example."

Shock ran through her. Had Melinda really just alluded to Blake…as a *benefactor*? "I'm not… That's not what I'm doing."

"No? Well, what are you doing then?" Melinda opened a manila folder on her desk. "Here, for example. Bent over his couch."

She flushed hot and then cold. Oh God. Her heart in her throat, she inched forward in the seat and peered over the desk. Sure enough, there she was. The image was taken through both blinds and curtains, revealing a naked woman in a most compromising position.

"How dare you?" she breathed.

"How dare I, Erin? No. How dare you sleep around with a professor just to make your grade. I saw that you have an A in his class right now."

"I earned that."

"The same way you earned A's in your other classes?"

"The exact same way. With my academic work."

"I suppose the rest is just extra credit." When Erin didn't answer, Melinda continued. "I can't fault you for trying. You get a good grade and land a hefty bank account to wipe out this debt. You're clearly a smart girl to get this far."

Horribly, she felt tears smart her eyes. She took a deep breath and forced them back.

"But now you can understand why I'm so worried about you. It's my responsibility to look out for the students…and to report immoral behavior by our staff."

"He didn't do anything."

She picked up the photograph and squinted. "Can he not get it up anymore? I wondered about that, after the accident. It does seem like a waste to have you all spread out and—"

"Just stop." Her stomach rolled. She was going to be sick.

"Look, I don't *want* to tell anyone. Realistically, the consequences will be more severe for him than for you. You'll maybe have to stay another semester and retake that class. But him? Everyone would know. What little life he has left right now would be ruined."

"What do you want?" she bit out.

"I don't think Professor Morris needs to hear from you outside class again, don't you think? Surely he has better things to do with his time."

Like you? she wanted to ask. But she couldn't. It wasn't funny. The joke was on her. Because Blake really could do anything and anyone. Whereas she was held hostage in this goddamned office. Whereas she had made all these god-damned *plans* to be successful and rich so that no one could push her around, yet here she was. Being pushed around. Weak. Helpless.

Melinda kept talking, but Erin could no longer hear her. She had mentally checked out, and besides, she already knew the gist of the message. *Go away. You're not wanted. You're not good enough.* The rushing sound in her ears was the same as when she'd been at her boyfriend's house. When his parents had cut her down over the soup course and told her she wasn't good enough then either.

After, she stumbled down the hall into her advisor's office.

Dr. Miller frowned at her. "Is everything okay? You're usually so punctual."

She just shook her head, at a loss. Relief washed through her when he took his seat behind his desk. Maybe she could go through the motions and make it through this meeting.

"I've got to be honest with you, Erin. We've talked about your work in-depth, and you know I'm very impressed. But I've also discussed it with one of the committee members and they've brought up some concerns…"

Oh God. She was completely sure who that

committee member was. She fumbled through the questions, on the defensive as she countered multiple arguments against her work. Some of them were legitimate concerns, weaknesses that she'd already addressed or had noted to revisit. Others were bogus, but she wasn't sure she was making a good case for herself anyway.

This wasn't the actual defense in front of the committee, but how much worse would that be? Dr. Miller already thought she was smart, that much was clear from the way he spoke to her. As if he was truly curious about her answers. It wouldn't be that way in front of the committee, with Melinda there. Who knew how far she'd gone to shore up support with the other committee members either? At the end of the two hours, an hour longer than they usually met, the best thing she could say about it was that she hadn't thrown up.

He took off his glasses. "There's one last thing. I really shouldn't even tell you this, but I like you, Erin. I think you have promise. So I'm making an exception. There's also been an accusation of plagiarism."

The air felt too thin. She was dizzy from it, nauseous. "What?"

"It hasn't been substantiated, and nothing will

happen unless it is. But if there's anything you want to tell me, now's the time."

Oh God, this was a nightmare. A true nightmare. "No. I came up with this, all of it. The only references I used are listed here."

He studied her for long minutes. Finally he nodded. "Then there shouldn't be a problem. I must admit, I was skeptical that you would do such a thing."

"I would never."

"No." He seemed thoughtful. "I don't think you would."

"Please, what's going to happen?"

"Quite frankly, if this situation is what I think it is, nothing. The only way the committee would act is if there's clear proof. Generally that is provided at the time the accusation is made."

But not this time, she understood. She managed to take her leave without completely falling to pieces and embarrassing herself. Two buildings away, she found Blake's door. The frosted window etched with his name was dark, the office empty. Relief was cold and tight in her belly. At least she could be alone for this. She sat down on the chair outside his office, the same one where she'd waited for him those weeks ago. Then she'd met him inside. Now she scribbled a note.

Can't do this anymore. Too risky. I'm sorry.
– E

Other words wanted to be written. *Love you, miss you. Help me.* But she didn't dare. The break needed to be clean, or she risked Melinda's wrath. And maybe this was for the best. It was Blake's reputation. His career. And hers. Their love wasn't worth risking those things, was it? She didn't know. Ironically, she wished she could talk it out with Blake. He always seemed to know what to do, always had the answers.

No, she needed to stand on her own. She couldn't protect him from his painful past. She couldn't protect him from an uphill future. But she could do this, now.

It was her own fault. That thought remained forefront in her mind, from the moment she'd realized Melinda knew the truth—no, before that. When Melinda had approached him and he hadn't been free to accept. He'd already been embroiled with Erin. What a nasty word, embroiled. Like a torrid affair, but that was what they had. A secret, forbidden relationship. And now? They had nothing.

She drove home on autopilot where she found her roommate still awake watching *House* reruns. Courtney held her while she cried and told her in halting, broken breaths what had happened.

Losing Blake… God, he was so much to her. Everything to her. But if he were found out now, shunned and ridiculed after so recently venturing out, he might never try again. He might never recover. And her own career, professional and otherwise, hung in the balance.

"Did I do the right thing?" Erin whispered.

Courtney's eyes were filled with sympathy. "Of course you did. There's a reason they don't allow those relationships. They just…don't work out."

Ah, the voice of rationality. Not entirely welcome at a time like this. She could hear Blake's rational voice too. His story about the Roman advisor who gave two hollow warnings to the Carthaginians before letting his true intentions show. He had never meant to leave them in peace. It had always, always been war.

Grimly, she acknowledged that the Romans had been so blithely aggressive because they could be. They held all the power, and so did Melinda. She made her fake ploy of being concerned about Erin and then called her a prostitute. And Erin had sat there and taken it. That was what she hated most of all. If she was going to go down, at least she could have put up a fight.

Chapter Sixteen

Blake

BLAKE SAT IN the dark, one knee crossed over the other. He rubbed the torn scrap of notebook paper between his finger and thumb. He didn't need to see to know what it said. *Can't do this anymore. Too risky.*

I'm sorry.

At first he'd only stared at the scribbled words in familiar handwriting. He couldn't process it. He *knew* her, damn it. This wasn't her. So what the fuck was it? He was going to find out.

The soft scraping sound of metal against metal came from the door as a key was turned. A sliver of moonlight beamed onto the knotted oak floor then disappeared again. Heels clicked, bags were shuffled. A lamp was turned on with a resounding click, revealing Blake's location in the armchair.

Melinda shrieked. "Oh, Blake. Jesus Christ. What are you doing?"

He stood, slipping the note into his pocket. "I

figured if my key still worked then yours would too. I suppose that's the price we pay for not ending things properly the first time around."

Her eyes narrowed at his clipped tone. Then a bright smile bloomed on her face. "Here to make amends? Don't worry that I'll make you beg, darling. I'm just happy to see you."

"Cut the bullshit. We both know why I'm here. After today."

The façade fell. She rolled her eyes. "What story did she tell you?"

"She didn't tell me anything about you, but you just confirmed it for me. What did you tell *her*? Did you threaten to vote down her thesis?"

"Well, whatever I said, it clearly worked, didn't it? So she couldn't have cared very much about you."

"No, let's see. I bet you threatened *me*. And now I'm supposed to believe that you care."

Finally she looked flustered. "Blake, I'm just trying to help. She's all wrong for you. Anyone can see that."

He advanced on her. Her eyes widened. She backed up until she hit the wall, causing the framed black-and-white photographs to shudder.

"Listen to me very carefully. I've tried asking nicely. I thought that would be enough. So let me put this in terms you understand. Leave her alone, or you'll regret it."

She scoffed, but her lower lip trembled. "What can you do to me? I'm the more senior professor. The permanent one. You're only temporary."

"I think the dean would be very interested to know about the rejection letter that magically fell off your records. What made them change their minds only a month later? And wasn't it generous of your father to pay for a new wing for the sociology building?"

Even in the dim light, he could see her grow pale. Some of the anger slipped off her face. "I didn't think you knew about that."

"Yeah, well, I can put two and two together. I didn't want to know, though. Like you said, we were both young and stupid. We don't have that excuse anymore. So don't you dare speak to her about academic integrity. Don't you dare speak to her about anything."

She closed her eyes. "Blake, we could be so good together. Don't you see it? I would stand by your side. Remember how we used to talk about that? I'm not afraid of a strong man, of being the woman behind one. That was our plan."

"Plans change, Mel. People change. For what

it's worth, I told you that I wanted to make a difference. And you said—"

"I said I would make that difference even bigger."

"Is this what we're supposed to be doing, bickering over a fucking semester? We won't be together, but we can find that spirit again. Of doing things that matter. Not harassing a young woman who's had a hard enough time as it is."

To her credit, Melinda looked contrite. "Really, I don't know where you even found her. I can't imagine she runs in our circles."

"Leave her alone, Mel. I know you're on the committee. You can challenge her all you want, but when it comes to vote, I expect you to do what you would for any other student. And since Reese Miller has been bragging about her project to any faculty who will listen, I have no doubt about the merits of her work. Are we clear?"

"My, my. You certainly get protective where this girl's involved. I guess it is more than an easy f—"

"Melinda."

"Fine. I'll leave her alone. And you'll keep my secret." She bent down and rummaged in her leather briefcase, pulling out a manila folder.

He accepted it and flipped it open. Jesus.

There was Erin, naked. His pulse pounded. "You came to my house," he said flatly.

"No, absolutely not. You told me not to." A pause. "I hired a private investigator. Oh, don't look at me like that. He didn't go on your property. He has one of those fancy long-distance-lens things."

He shut his eyes and took a deep breath. The sad part was, he wasn't even surprised. Just angry. They may have been young and stupid, possibly still were, but Erin was light years ahead of them. Mature and brave. He was furious she'd had to face this alone. Hurt that she hadn't come to him for help.

I'm sorry, she'd said. Well, fuck, he was sorry too. But he would fix this. He'd fix every single thing that came up, run a goddamn gauntlet if she needed him to until she finally believed in them.

ERIN

SHE'D JUST GOTTEN out of the shower when her phone rang. She dried herself off quickly and grabbed it, thinking *Blake* and *no, not Blake.* Her stomach sank. Her mother.

"Hey, Mom."

"What's wrong?" her mother asked immediately.

"How do you know anything's wrong?"

"Oh, sweetie, I've known. You haven't been calling as much, and now your nose sounds stuffy. Either you've caught a head cold, or you've been crying."

Her smile pushed away some of the clouds she'd felt all afternoon. "You know me too well."

"Talk to me."

It was probably time to give it up, anyway. There was nowhere to go from here, nothing to be gained from discretion. She sighed.

"I made a mistake. A big one." Or several, depending on the way she portioned it out. "I was seeing someone. He was in the military but he'd left. And then he got an offer from the university and accepted it before we knew...before we knew he'd be teaching my class. My last class. By then it was too late to back out."

"Oh, Erin. I can't believe..."

She laughed shortly, understanding the speechlessness all too well. "Yes. Now it looks like we might be found out. Almost. So I've broken things off with him."

What a thin phrase for what she felt. Broken things off, as if it were a twig from a tree. Instead of how she felt—shattered. Split apart into a thousand shards. Her stomach clenched tight, her head strangely thick and full of cotton. Not all of this came from leaving that note for Blake. Some was the humiliation of being accused of whoring herself, as she sat in an office in her university. She'd felt so low, so unworthy. How she'd always felt, really, but all her insecurity had floated to the surface. Her eyes closed tightly. In fact, maybe that was why she'd been so damn quick to write that note. She'd felt awful, disgusting, and she hadn't wanted to tell Blake about that. Hadn't wanted to see him defend her, knowing that she probably deserved the censure. Or worse—hadn't wanted to see the light of agreement in his eyes.

"Of course you did the right thing ending it," her mother said.

Erin said nothing.

"In fact, I... A professor, Erin? How old is he?"

"Not that old. It's not like he was tenured or anything. Just a man with a graduate degree and a good academic reputation who they've hired for the semester."

"I don't understand. If you didn't meet him through the university, where did you?"

Her stomach clenched. She took a deep breath. "I was cleaning his house."

"Erin!"

"I'm sorry, Mom, but I just… It wasn't a big deal." A lie, of course. It had been a huge deal, and she'd known her mother would mind that most of all.

"Erin, men like that—"

"You don't even know him."

"I know enough. Men like that don't respect women who clean their big, expensive houses."

"Blake's not like that."

"Oh, so he's not rich? He didn't grow up with everything handed to him?"

"God. Not all rich people are like that."

There was silence on the other end of the phone. They both knew what Erin meant. Whatever unspoken thing had been done to her mother by the man she worked for.

When she spoke again, her mother's voice had softened into pleading. "Tell me this much. Did he ask you out, take you on a nice date like he can afford? Or did he make a move while you were working and suggest that you keep it a secret?"

She felt like she might throw up. She was just so confused, so upset. She didn't really doubt Blake, but it was hard to explain. What could she say? *I caught him masturbating and thought it would be fun to join in.* That would hardly make her mother feel better. Besides, Blake had his own reasons for being so reclusive, and she didn't want to get into that now.

As much as she disagreed with her mother's assessment, she could also understand her worry. From the outside, it looked similar. Goddamned precedent. For reasons she couldn't explain it made her angry to use Blake's lesson in this, but she couldn't ignore the implications. Her mother was the precedent here, the framework for analyzing her own situation. But in this case, the differences were so vital, so deep at the core, that it turned the precedent on its head. Her mother's boss had taken advantage of his position. Blake was her friend. Her lover. And he didn't deserve to be tossed away like garbage because she suddenly got scared. Even if she had a good reason to be scared.

She sighed. "I'll work it out, Mom. Don't worry."

"Baby…"

"What about you? How are your knees?"

Her mother's harrumph told her she didn't appreciate the blatant attempt at distraction. "They're fine. I'm always fine as long as my little girl is okay."

She placated her mother with promises that

she would focus on school and take care of herself. Which she would, but that included talking to Blake. Once she was tucked into bed, her tears fell freely. Melinda's words kept replaying in her mind. *I suppose the rest is just extra credit.* God. What a bad day, that was all she could think. What a horrible day, and the one man who could make her feel better, she'd pushed away. She cried until she was exhausted and sleep finally overtook her.

In the morning her eyes were puffy. She felt tired and tense at the same time. A jog would loosen her muscles at least. She dressed quickly, throwing on her ratty workout clothes and graying sneakers. But when she opened the front door of her apartment, she stopped cold.

A small cardboard box sat in the alcove. Her body felt wooden as she knelt to look inside. A few of her books were stacked at the bottom. A sweatshirt. And a note. She unfolded it with shaking hands.

Don't worry about M. I took care of it. Love you.

He'd written a note instead of trying to talk to her, exactly as she'd done to him. He'd come to her apartment and left this box of her things. A chill ran down her spine. If it were really over between them, if he was done with her...

Love you, he'd written. Two little words, and she hung every last one of her hopes on them.

ERIN

ERIN STARED AT the wide farmhouse.

The shutters were green. How had she never noticed that before?

The engine was probably cool by now. She suspected he knew she was out here, but he hadn't come out. Wouldn't come out. The note had made that much clear. He was going to quietly go away because she'd asked him to. God. She hated herself. Was he pissed at her? He should be. Strangely, she was pissed at him for respecting her request, since he seemed to know about Melinda's threats. Didn't he know she'd been desperate and distraught? Didn't he care?

Well, she would speak to him today. He deserved that much. So here she was, gathering up the courage to go inside. Trying to figure out whether she would ask for him back or just give him the closure he deserved.

With a sigh, she stepped out of the car and went to the door. He answered after only a minute, confirming her suspicion that he knew she was out there. That he knew how hard this was for her. His expression was reserved, eyes revealing nothing. None of the hot desire he usually let her see. None of the love. The anxiety in her stomach grew heavier. Her heart beat faster.

"Good morning," he said, and what did that even mean? She felt anxious and not totally put back together after her little breakdown.

"Morning."

He stepped back to let her in. She couldn't take her eyes off him as she passed. The green T-shirt he wore hung off his broad shoulders, loose where his waist narrowed. His jeans rested on his hips and sloped over muscular thighs. He was barefoot and smelling of soap…in a word, edible. But he wasn't hers, because she'd panicked. Because she'd caved.

She turned to face him. "You look good." A blush heated her cheeks. She hadn't meant to say that.

He quirked that lopsided smile. "That's one benefit of looking like I do. A few shadows under my eyes don't make much of an impact. I couldn't sleep."

Her breath caught. "Blake. I'm sorry."

"Yes, I read that in your note." There was a

reserve to his voice, making him foreign and intimidating. Not the Blake she'd lain in bed with. Not even the Blake who'd chatted with her when she came to clean his house.

"I freaked out. I made a mistake."

"We all have our moments." His words were forgiving. His tone was not.

She stared at him. "So, that's it?"

"If that's all you want, then yes. For now." He was still courteous. Still cold.

"What do you mean *for now*?"

"I mean I'm not going to push you. This semester. There's a few weeks left. If you don't want to see me during them, I'll respect that."

She made a face. "And if I don't want to see you after that?"

"You will."

Hope bloomed inside her, fast and powerful. "You sound very sure of yourself."

"I'm a work in progress, but this much I know, you want me. I want you. Nothing's going to change that."

She frowned. "How did you know what happened?"

"About Melinda? Because you aren't the kind of woman to cut and run. It hurt like hell to get that note. Even Melinda said her goodbye face-to-face."

Guilt squeezed her throat, making it hard to breathe. Tears pricked at her eyes, but she blinked them away. She'd hurt him worse than she thought. Imagining herself so very different, so much better than Melinda and then doing the same thing. Worse.

"I'm so sorry," she whispered.

He looked over at the windows, where thick cream-colored drapes blocked the view. Now those were definitely new. He had been busy.

"It didn't make sense, though, for you to do it. You've told me so many times you don't care about how I look—"

"I *love* how you look," she interrupted.

He smiled slightly. "Sometimes I just like hearing you repeat it."

"Nice."

"I knew you wouldn't leave because of that or because things were difficult. Unless you got scared about something. By someone."

She groaned. "I never should have freaked out like that."

"It's okay. We all get freaked out sometimes. I think I hold the world's record for longest time spent hiding in his house."

"That was different. You were…" She

couldn't say the words. Almost killed. A prisoner of war.

"Wounded," he said softly.

She swallowed hard. He'd never really talked about what had happened before, and she'd never pushed. He pulled her to the couch and sat down with her. She remembered, with a flash of heat, what they'd done on this couch with a glass of wine. His smile said he noticed her blush.

He grew serious. "I was upset you didn't come talk to me when Melinda threatened you. Did you think I'd get pissed at you?"

"No," she said quickly. "It's not that. I wasn't thinking straight and I wanted to handle it myself. I feel like I'm always coming to you with problems or trying to change you. I was the one who pushed you into accepting the job and then it got all twisted when we found out it was my class."

"Erin, only I can take responsibility for the things I did. Or the things I didn't do. That's something I've had to relearn recently. I accepted the position because I thought it was the right thing to do. I'm not going to let Melinda jeopardize that any more than I'm going to let her come between us."

She narrowed her eyes. "So how exactly did

you take care of it?"

He shrugged. "Oh, the usual. Blackmail, extortion. Now that I think of it, I could have used bribery. But it didn't come to that."

"Blake Morris, you didn't! The pillar of honor and integrity."

"Don't pin those words on me, sweetheart. I was raised to be a politician, remember? Besides, it got the job done. And this isn't about you bringing me problems or trying to change me. This is taking care of what's mine."

She felt breathless, her body alight with excitement. "I'm yours?"

"You know the answer to that, Erin. You're mine forever, whether I touch you in three minutes or three weeks or three years. Though let's not wait as long as that last one, please."

"Touch me now," she whispered. She wanted to feel connected to him again, the deep and abiding intimacy that only came of bodies joining.

He raised an eyebrow. "Are you sure?"

"Yes. Please."

"If I take you, we're going upstairs to my bed, and I'm not letting you out until morning. You're going to be very sore tomorrow."

She moaned softly, imagining all the ways they would fill those hours. Her body twinged with the phantom imprint of him, eager for the thick length filling her up.

"Are you thirsty?" he asked solicitously. "Hungry? We should take care of you now. You'll need to keep up your strength."

Her groan was pure sexual frustration. "You're teasing me."

"A little payback, sweetheart. You really drove me crazy with that note." He still spoke evenly, but she sensed the turmoil beneath his words, how deeply she'd affected him.

CHAPTER SEVENTEEN

ERIN

SHE TOOK HIS hands in hers, marveling at how large they were, how strong and capable they felt. And yet he let her hold them, turn them over. Let her press her lips to the back of his hand. He was like that everywhere, big and wonderfully competent, yet he allowed her to lead. Was it because he knew she needed that? Or a natural respect he granted her as his lover? There was so much more she wanted to know about him.

It wasn't seductive, but it was honest. "What happened over there? You don't have to tell me everything. I wouldn't expect that. Just…something I don't know."

He didn't seem surprised by her question. He nodded, as if it were the most natural thing in the world for her to ask about his darkest hour, and maybe it was.

"We were on patrol. Me and three other guys. We were attacked by insurgents with missile launchers. Taken by surprised and outgunned. One of my men died on impact."

Her breath caught. His voice was flat, but God, the pain wavered near the surface. She could feel it in the air around her. It shimmered there, like a hot summer's day.

"Joe was trapped under the vehicle. I want to take you to visit him someday soon, by the way. We knew they were coming for us, but I was messed up too badly from the explosion to move. The last guy though…he got up and walked away. I watched him go. First he walked, then he took off running. I was furious with him for leaving us that way, but at the same time…envious." He laughed hollowly. "I wanted to be the hell away from there."

"Oh, Blake." She heard what he didn't say. One of his teammates had walked away. When he'd gotten home, his fiancée had walked away. *This* was his nightmare. His worst fear was being left behind. And she'd triggered that. She pressed a kiss to the center of his palm, as if she could draw the pain inside of her, just breathe it in.

"I found out later he was never recovered. Presumed dead. So what's the lesson there, huh? Walk away and die of starvation. Or stay behind and get tortured—" He broke off at her small gasp. "I'm sorry, I didn't mean to go that far. It feels so random. So horribly random."

Her heart broke for him. He was a scholar, so goddamned intelligent he couldn't see the writing on the wall. He wanted answers to life's tragedies when their very unfair nature meant they had none. A life that allowed a strong, loyal protector to be slain and left for dead. That allowed a hardworking woman like her mother to suffer and be victimized, all for what? She certainly couldn't comprehend it or explain, but it was true nonetheless.

"I don't know why these things happen," she confessed. "I'm not sure we can understand."

He stared at her for a moment. "Well, that's the most depressing thing I've ever heard."

She laughed suddenly, because even though the situation was serious and fraught, it seemed ironic. That he had seen and lived through unimaginable things—things like torture and treason—only to find her comment depressing.

He laughed too, with a teasing glint in his eyes. "Okay, my little philosopher. Why are we here then?"

She was going to make a joke about fatalism being the better part of valor, but she paused. Because she knew the answer, at least the one she lived by. Grasping his wrist, she drew his hand to her heart. His palm nestled above her breasts, but this wasn't sexual. Her hand spread over his chest, feeling the steady thump beneath. His eyes widened slightly.

"This," she said softly. The things they discussed in class, those constructs and mores that drew invisible arrows between ideas, that supported one conclusion and empirically disproved another…yes, they were interesting. Stimulating. A worthwhile pursuit in the bright hours of the day. But they paled in comparison to the deep and enduring connection between him and her, a safe place to rest when the night cast the world in shadows.

She could live on the power coursing between them. She could thrive on it. If that made her less of an intellectual, she accepted that, because she knew what she felt. She still wanted to be successful, but not at the expense of her heart.

That was why she'd come back to him. She'd rather lose her degree than give up the magic she'd found with him. She'd rather stand at his side than live in chains made of fear and ambition.

His gaze was hard and tender at the same time. "Considering I'm the professor between us, I have a lot to learn from you."

She blushed. He smiled and reached up to touch her heated skin.

"Be with me?" she whispered uncertainly. An apology and entreaty all at once. Not everything was solved and sorted between them, but then they never would be. Like the eddies and entrapments of life, they could only face each obstacle as it came. No promise of smooth waters, just a partner for the journey.

His eyes softened. "You never have to ask, lovely. I'm here. Wherever you go and whenever you come back, I'm yours."

They leaned forward at the same time, their lips pressed together, bodies fusing. The air was sucked out of the room. She opened her mouth against his, drawing her breath from him, taking sustenance and feeding it back. Her tongue flicked into his mouth, and he groaned.

"Upstairs," he muttered. "No more sex on the sofa for a while."

She laughed but complied, preceding him up the stairs. "I saw the new window dressings."

"Not good enough. I'm going to buy up all the land around here too. Or maybe I can find an island. We'll make a country for just the two of us."

"And you'll be the king?" Reaching his bedroom, she climbed onto his bed.

"Yes," he said, making quick work of his clothes.

Her mouth went dry at the sight of his naked body, the hard planes sprinkled with dark male hair. The erect length that rose between his legs. "And I'll be the queen?"

"You'll be my subject. The first ordinance, no clothes on you. Ever." He approached her and tugged off her shirt, her bra. Pulled her to stand and didn't stop until she was naked.

"What about when we have guests? Surely I should wear clothes then."

"We don't permit visas," he said apologetically. "Second ordinance. Everything you do must be in pursuit of pleasure."

She walked herself back on the bed while he followed. "This all seems very restrictive."

"I might let you leave occasionally. Once a day. To work and back."

"And yoga class?"

"Is it self-serving for me to agree to that one too? It makes me so hot how flexible you are."

She grinned. "And an occasional girls' night out?"

"All these questions, this civil unrest," he murmured against her neck. His lips skated over her collarbone, igniting nerves all over her body.

She shivered. "Maybe I'll have a rebellion."

"Ah, but you already rule me. Anything else is just a game we play."

BLAKE

BLAKE ALLOWED HER to flip them over. She grasped his hands in hers, pinning him to the bed. Her curves were pale and tantalizing. He could do nothing but stare at her, entranced by the sight of her.

Her strength held him down too. Not the physical force of her palms against his or her slender thighs straddling his but that indomitable will of hers. Threatened, but she pushed forward anyway. Uncertain, but she laid her heart open to him.

She had humbled him downstairs. *This*, she'd said, connecting their hearts with their hands. And he'd known she was right. He'd *felt* she was right, but he wasn't sure he'd have been able to find this place without her. It was like wandering a forest for years, only to have her take him by the hand and lead him to a cool, running stream. It had been here all along, he'd just been too blind to find it.

She nipped at the line of his jaw. The pinch slid down his spine and burrowed itself into his balls. He bucked his hips, rubbing his cock between the damp folds of her sex.

"Jesus, woman."

Her smile left no doubt that she knew her own power. It was potent sexuality. It was peace. He grasped her hands where they held his down, dying without being able to touch her and more than willing. This was the stuff of wet dreams, her body spread open to his hungry gaze, his held down for her pleasure.

"Use me," he said hoarsely. "Fuck me."

She bit her lip. "Not like that."

"How then?"

She released him, supporting herself with the bed and half entwined with him. He immediately ran his hands along the slope of her back, admiring her smoothness, embracing her. A sensual roll of her hips and she hovered over him, the head of his cock hitched to her opening. He gritted his teeth to fight the piercing desire to thrust upward, holding his body flat against the bed. Slowly, achingly, she lowered herself to him, around him, enveloping him in softness and scalding him with exquisite heat.

Her eyes remained on his through the entire

downward slide and beyond. Even when she began to move over him in a sumptuous undulation, her warm gaze was locked with his. He drowned in those eyes, those amber pools of desire and acceptance. She looked deep inside him and found him worthy; he tithed with his body, his soul, for a chance to make her come. The ripples around his cock meant she was close, but her expression was solemn, focused. Steady.

It wasn't the right rhythm to make him come, not fast enough really, but he was glad of it. This way he could last. Even her gorgeous body and the poignant feel of her couldn't overcome biology. The slow grind was a communion, a prayer—a goddamned miracle. He swallowed thickly. If he fondled her clit or sucked her nipples, she would clench around him in seconds, but he found himself reluctant to end this quickly. He wanted to watch her come at her own pace, to take her own pleasure. He wanted to suffer in wait.

Her breasts pressed to his chest, and he knew she was rubbing her clit against his body. He was hard and aching in the clasp of her body, trembling with restraint. Her movements became smaller, more specific, rocking her hips over him, fucking him.

She was taking from him, her pleasure, his power, and he was hollow from it, open. There wasn't a single thing he'd hold back from her—not love, not sex. Not surrender.

"Blake. Blake." She was calling for him, sounding lost and afraid, staring into his eyes.

"I'm here, baby. Fuck, I'm right here." His voice was like grit in the air around them, rough and unruly.

He felt a tightening of her inner muscles as she clamped down around him. A rush of hot liquid coated his cock. His eyes narrowed to slits, but he couldn't close them, couldn't look away—fuck, he couldn't look away from the sight of her in climax, her face slack and open and so damned lovely. So lovely.

He came. She was completely still over him, frozen at the peak, but he was coming in long, painful drags, emptying himself into her body, finding completion and so much more. There was nothing sweeter than the feel of her falling apart in his arms, needing him, *trusting* him—of finally trusting himself.

Trusting himself to do what was right, what was necessary, even if it wasn't what he wanted. Her inner muscles flexed around him, and he forced himself to roll them over, to pull away from her. He pushed the hair away from her face, cradling her cheek.

"Erin," he murmured. "I think we should stop seeing each other."

Her body went rigid beneath his, sensual pleasure draining from her eyes. "What?"

He dealt with Melinda, but she was only a symptom of the problem. She would never have been able to threaten Erin if Blake hadn't been with her. "Baby, I love you more than life. And I love you enough to let you go. How can I stand behind a podium and teach about ethics, without living it myself?"

She sat up, dragging a sheet to cover herself. Already he was losing her, even if it was only the sight of her pink-tipped breasts. It felt like losing a limb. A vital organ.

He had to make the sever complete.

"We talked about this," she said, her voice wavery. "You didn't force me to do anything. And I stopped working for you. Isn't that enough? That should be enough."

"I know I didn't mean to force you. And I know you didn't feel forced, but that doesn't change the fact that I was your employer at the time. That I became your professor. I should know more than anyone that the ends don't justify the means."

"Blake, don't do this to us. It's just a little bit longer."

"And maybe then…" He forced himself to stop, not to give her false hope, not to sway her decision in any way. She needed to be free to graduate without a barrier, to choose her path without taking him into account. If she found her way back to him he would be grateful beyond reason, he would fall down at her feet, but he could not ask her to stay.

It took a strength of will he wasn't sure he had to pull away from the bed and walk to the closet. To pull on a pair of sweatpants as if that could negate what they'd just done. "No, not even then, Erin. You have your whole life ahead of you. That life doesn't include me."

It felt like stepping on an IED all over again, the shock to his system, the physical pain the bloomed across his body. The blinding reality that nothing would ever be the same.

THE END

Thank you so much for reading BEAUTY AND THE PROFESSOR.

He can never turn back into a prince... A trouble revelation puts Blake's newfound career in jeopardy—and even worse, puts Erin's impending graduate at risk. He can't risk her future no matter how much he wants her. Read FALLING FOR THE BEAST now!

She will never have a happily ever after...

A dark legacy threatens everything they've worked to build. When old debt comes between them, both Blake and Erin must fight to protect each other—and their love.

Since their forbidden beginning, Erin and Blake's relationship has been marked by deep sensuality and intense emotion. The couple is tested at every turn. They're running out of time. Blake and Erin will have to trust each other to forge their own sexy ending.

"Their story is not only very memorable and extremely sexy, but I could read this series

many times over and never tire of it."

—Ms Romantic Reads

And don't miss the brand new release!

Forbidden fruit never tasted this sweet...

"Swoon-worthy, forbidden, and sexy, Liam North is my new obsession."

—New York Times bestselling author
Claire Contreras

The world knows Samantha Brooks as the violin prodigy. She guards her secret truth—the desire she harbors for her guardian.

Liam North got custody of her six years ago. She's all grown up now, but he still treats her like a child. No matter how much he wants her.

No matter how bad he aches for one taste.

"Overture is a beautiful composition of forbidden love and undeniable desire. Skye has crafted a gripping, sensual, and intense story that left me breathless. Get ready to be hooked!"

—USA Today bestselling author
Nikki Sloane

Turn the page for an excerpt from OVER-TURE...

EXCERPT FROM OVERTURE

*R*EST, LIAM TOLD me.

He's right about a lot of things. Maybe he's right about this. I climb onto the cool pink sheets, hoping that a nap will suddenly make me content with this quiet little life.

Even though I know it won't.

Besides, I'm too wired to actually sleep. The white lace coverlet is both delicate and comfy. It's actually what I would have picked out for myself, except I didn't pick it out. I've been incapable of picking anything, of choosing anything, of deciding anything as part of some deep-seated fear that I'll be abandoned.

The coverlet, like everything else in my life, simply appeared.

And the person responsible for its appearance? Liam North.

I climb under the blanket and stare at the ceiling. My body feels overly warm, but it still feels good to be tucked into the blankets. The blankets *he* picked out for me.

It's really so wrong to think of him in a sexual way. He's my guardian, literally. Legally. And he has never done anything to make me think he sees *me* in a sexual way.

This is it. This is the answer.

I don't need to go skinny dipping in the lake down the hill. Thinking about Liam North in a sexual way is my fast car. My parachute out of a plane.

My eyes squeeze shut.

That's all it takes to see Liam's stern expression, those fathomless green eyes and the glint of dark blond whiskers that are always there by late afternoon. And then there's the way he touched me. My forehead, sure, but it's more than he's done before. That broad palm on my sensitive skin.

My thighs press together. They want something between them, and I give them a pillow. Even the way I masturbate is small and timid, never making a sound, barely moving at all, but I can't change it now. I can't moan or throw back my head even for the sake of rebellion.

But I can push my hips against the pillow, rocking my whole body as I imagine Liam doing more than touching my forehead. He would trail his hand down my cheek, my neck, my shoulder.

Repressed. I'm so repressed it's hard to imagine more than that.

I make myself do it, make myself trail my hand down between my breasts, where it's warm and velvety soft, where I imagine Liam would know exactly how to touch me.

You're so beautiful, he would say. *Your breasts are perfect.*

Because Imaginary Liam wouldn't care about big breasts. He would like them small and soft with pale nipples. That would be the absolute perfect pair of breasts for him.

And he would probably do something obscene and rude. Like lick them.

My hips press against the pillow, almost pushing it down to the mattress, rocking and rocking. There's not anything sexy or graceful about what I'm doing. It's pure instinct. Pure need.

The beginning of a climax wraps itself around me. Claws sink into my skin. There's almost certain death, and I'm fighting, fighting, fighting for it with the pillow clenched hard.

"Oh fuck."

The words come soft enough someone else might not hear them. They're more exhalation of breath, the consonants a faint break in the sound.

I have excellent hearing. Ridiculous, crazy good hearing that had me tuning instruments before I could ride a bike.

My eyes snap open, and there's Liam, standing there, frozen. Those green eyes locked on mine. His body clenched tight only three feet away from me. He doesn't come closer, but he doesn't leave.

Orgasm breaks me apart, and I cry out in surprise and denial and relief. "*Liam.*"

It goes on and on, the terrible pleasure of it. The wrenching embarrassment of coming while looking into the eyes of the man who raised me for the past six years.

Want to read more? OVERTURE is available on Amazon, iBooks, Barnes & Noble, Kobo, and other book retailers!

MORE BOOKS BY SKYE WARREN

Endgame trilogy & Masterpiece Duet

The Pawn

The Knight

The Castle

The King

The Queen

Trust Fund Duet

Survival of the Richest

The Evolution of Man

North Security series

Overture

Concerto

Underground series

Rough

Hard

Fierce

Wild

Dirty

Secret

Sweet

Deep

Stripped series

Tough Love

Love the Way You Lie

Better When It Hurts

Even Better

Pretty When You Cry

Caught for Christmas

Hold You Against Me

To the Ends of the Earth

Standalone Books

Wanderlust

On the Way Home

Beauty and the Beast

Anti Hero

Escort

ABOUT THE AUTHOR

Skye Warren is the New York Times bestselling author of contemporary romance such as the Chicago Underground and Stripped series. Her books have been featured in Jezebel, Buzzfeed, USA Today Happily Ever After, Glamour, and Elle Magazine. She makes her home in Texas with her loving family, two sweet dogs, and one evil cat.

Sign up for Skye's newsletter:
www.skyewarren.com/newsletter

Like Skye Warren on Facebook:
facebook.com/skyewarren

Join Skye Warren's Dark Room reader group:
skyewarren.com/darkroom

Follow Skye Warren on Instagram:
instagram.com/skyewarrenbooks

Visit Skye's website for her current booklist:
www.skyewarren.com/books

COPYRIGHT

Beauty and the Professor © 2019 by Skye Warren
Print Edition

Cover design by Steamy Designs
Formatted by BB eBooks

Printed in Great Britain
by Amazon